Rafe chuckled. "Lad_____
care about that stuff?"

She checked her line then slung a glance his way. "Since a certain doctor moved to town. That's when."

Huh? Did she mean what it sounded like she meant? Rafe sat up. "What are you talking about?"

She bit her bottom lip, and her big blue eyes studied him for a moment. "Promise you won't tell anyone?"

"What do I look like? Some gossipy old woman?" He shrugged. "Tell me or not. It doesn't matter to me."

"Sorry. Guess I'm a little fidgety talking about it." She hesitated, and a blush washed over her face. "Truth is, I'm kind of sweet on the new doctor."

Rafe tensed and took a deep breath. He managed a sharp laugh. "I see. So is he sweet on you, too?"

"How should I know? I've never even spoken to the man." Her face softened, and tenderness filled her eyes. Something he'd only seen on Tuck when she was talking about a new baby calf or something. "But he will be. I'll see to that."

A bolt of unexplainable anger shot through him. "Oh really? And how do you mean to go about it?"

"Not sure yet." She closed her eyes and sighed. "He's just about the handsomest man I've ever laid eyes on, Rafe. Hair black as midnight and deep, stormy blue eyes."

"You mean like Lexie's?"

She glared and gave a scornful laugh. "Of course not. The doctor's hair and eyes don't look like a woman's."

"Okay. Don't get so riled up. I get it."

She sighed. "I'm going to marry him, Rafe."

Rafe's chest tightened and a knot formed in his throat. He wasn't sure why, but he'd better do something before he exploded.

FRANCES DEVINE spent most of her childhood, teen, and young adult years in Dallas, Texas, but lived for five years in a little country community called Brushy Creek among the beautiful pine woods of East Texas. There, she wrote her first story at the age of nine. She moved to Southwest Missouri more than twenty years ago and fell in love with the hills, the fall colors, and Silver Dollar City. Frances considers herself blessed to have the opportunity to write for Barbour Books. She is the mother of seven adult children and has fourteen wonderful grandchildren. Frances is happy to hear from her fans. E-mail her at fd1440writes@aol.com.

Books by Frances Devine

HEARTSONG PRESENTS
HP847—A Girl Like That
HP871—Once a Thief
HP955—White River Dreams

White River Song

Frances Devine

Heartsong Presents

I'd like to dedicate this book to all the tomboys of the world and the families who wouldn't change them for anything. And to my own family. I love each of you more than I can express, and I can't imagine life without you.

Very special thanks to my Lord and Savior Jesus Christ, My All Sufficient One.

A note from the Author:
I love to hear from my readers! You may correspond with me by writing:

Frances Devine
Author Relations
PO Box 721
Uhrichsville, OH 44683

ISBN 978-1-61626-527-4

WHITE RIVER SONG

All scripture quotations are taken from the King James Version of the Bible.

This book is a work of fiction. Names, characters, places, and incidents are either products of the author's imagination or used fictitiously.

Our mission is to publish and distribute inspirational products offering exceptional value and biblical encouragement to the masses.

PRINTED IN THE U.S.A.

one

The note hung high in the air, sweet and mournful. Kentucky Sullivan perched on the rickety bench, her bow held high. She closed her eyes, allowing the tension to build, then, with a swing of her arm, drew the bow across the strings. The note, mixed with the sounds of banjo and accordion, plunged into an ear-splitting cacophony that sounded like a passel of pigs squealing. Maybe with some chicken squawking flung in for good measure. It never failed to amaze Tuck how the four of them could make beautiful music one minute then an agony of crazy squeaks and screeches the next. But there was no denying it was fun.

She flung herself against the front wall of the feed store by the mill, wincing as the rough boards stabbed at her shoulder blades, then grinned at her fellow musicians.

"Whew! That there was some good fiddling, Tuck." Mr. Willie Van Schultz slipped his fiddle under his arm then removed his slouchy hat to wipe a hand across his bald head. "Mighty good." He grinned and plopped the hat back in place.

"Well thanks, Mr. Willie. You sounded pretty fair to middling yourself." Her shock of thick braids bobbed as she nodded, several straw-colored strands escaping their confinement.

The old man laid his fiddle on the bench next to him and cackled. He'd taught Tuck nearly everything she knew about fiddling over the last decade, and they both knew she was nowhere near his match.

With a sigh, she wrapped the silk cloth around her instrument and placed it in the case. The handmade violin had come from Ireland with her great-grandfather many years ago. A final pat, and she closed the lid with gentle pressure. "I've got to get a move on."

"Ya sure ya gotta go, Tuck?"

The cracked voice brought a smile to Kentucky's face, and she grinned at Squeezebox Tanner, the best accordion player in the entire Ozarks. Or at least as far as Tuck's knowledge went, which was just about fifteen miles on either side of Branson. "Yes, Addy will be waiting for me at the general store." She shook her head. "If I'm late, she'll throw a fit."

"You sure you're talking about your sister? Fit throwing is more up your alley, ain't it?" Tom Black's laugh came out as a wheeze, and he quickly laid his banjo on the bench and bent over until the coughing spell was over.

Tuck shrugged. He was right. Her twin never threw fits. The old man's hacking cough started up again. She winced. "Maybe you should give up that corncob pipe of yours, Mr. Tom."

"And maybe you oughta' be mindin' yore own bizness, Miss Sullivan."

Tuck covered her mouth with her hand to hide the grin she couldn't hold back. "And maybe you're right. I should at that." Tucking her fiddle under her arm, she gave a jaunty wave, leaving them laughing as she pranced off down the dusty road toward Branson's General Store.

Her twin sister stood by the wagon tapping her toe and glaring as she watched Tuck walk toward her.

Uh-oh. Tuck crossed the road and cast a side grin at her sister. "Sorry. Guess I'm a few minutes late. I got all caught up with our practice."

"A few minutes? More like twenty while I stood a gazing stock for every passerby." Her frown spoke a thousand words, and the anger in her eyes was apparently meant to cut through Tuck like a knife.

"You could have waited inside." She groaned. She'd been trying to do better with sarcastic remarks since she got baptized two months ago. Lately, it was awful hard though when her sister was around. Addy used to be the sweetest thing in the world. A little too sweet in Tuck's opinion. What in tarnation had gotten into her? "Sorry. I sort of got lost in the music."

A most unladylike snort emitted from Addy's pretty little mouth. "Music. Humph. If that's what you want to call the noise you and those old fogies squeeze out of those horrid instruments."

All right. That was it. Tuck opened her mouth to retort but stopped as her sister leaned over and hissed in her ear. "Someone is approaching. Oh my goodness, Abby, your collar is tucked inside your dress." She dug her fingers into Tuck's neckline.

"I'll fix it, and don't call me Abby!" Tuck pushed her sister's hand away. "What are you so nervous about? I always tuck my collar in when I play the fiddle."

"Hush." Addy shushed her, the frown turning into a simpering smile, as a coquettish look appeared in the previously stormy eyes.

At the *clip-clop* of a horse on the hardened road, Tuck twisted around.

The stranger sat tall and relaxed in the saddle, a hint of a smile on his lips. Dark blue eyes danced as they rested on the two sisters. When he lifted his hand and touched the brim of his hat, a lock of dark hair fell across his forehead. "Afternoon, ladies."

Her breath exploded from her open mouth with a loud *whoosh*. Had someone just kicked her in the stomach? By the time Kentucky's pounding heart settled back to normal, horse and rider had rounded a curve in the road and disappeared behind a grove of oak trees. "Who was that?" Whoever he was, she was going to marry him.

A dreamy look crossed her sister's face. "The new doctor, Sam Fields, and I think he's going to be your new brother-in-law."

Tuck returned to her senses and frowned. Obviously, Addy was as bowled over by the doctor as she was. Huh. Her sister was in for a great big surprise.

"Abby, why are you looking at me like that?" A frown crossed Addy's face.

Okay, this wouldn't be easy. First, Tuck couldn't let on that she was smitten with the doctor. "I said don't call me Abby. My name is Kentucky. Do you hear?"

"All right. Don't get so riled up. But don't you think you're a little old for such a childish nickname?"

"No, I like it." Tuck glared at her sister. Miss Bossy.

Tuck scrambled up onto the wagon seat and grabbed the reins, barely waiting long enough for her sister to scurry onto the seat before she flicked the reins. "Hiiiya, Toby, Haystack."

The mules took off at a lumbered pace. Why couldn't they go faster? If she had to be this close to Addy much longer, she might explode. She turned and grabbed the long black whip from the back of the wagon. Papa Jack had made it for one of the neighbors to use in a stunt riding show and hadn't gotten around to taking it to the man yet. She cracked the whip, and the mules took off running.

"Abigail Sullivan! What do you think you're doing?" Addy grabbed at Tuck's arm and tried to wrestle the whip away. "Let go of it. Papa Jack will kill you if you hurt his mules."

So she wants me to let go? Fine. Tuck opened her hand and Addy fell backward, teetering close to the side. Tuck grabbed her by the arm and steadied her.

She pulled hard on the reins and brought the wagon to

a stop. Leaning over, she panted for breath, then finally sat up and stared at her sister. The look of horror on Addy's face struck Tuck as funny. A giggle rose from deep in her belly, exploding into great gulping, gasping laughter. "Hooo." Spent, she leaned back in the seat, her chest hurting.

"Look at me." Addy's voice was barely above a whisper.

The soft words surprised Tuck and she glanced at her sister. "What?"

"You like him, too, don't you?"

"What are you talking about? Like who?" Tuck knew the innocent tone wouldn't fool anyone, much less Addy.

"It's no use. I know you like him."

"So, what if I do?" Tuck frowned. She should have been more careful.

Addy picked up the reins and handed them to her. "Then you shall have him. Let's go home."

Tuck eyed her sister. Was she serious? Why did she always give up so easily? She flicked the reins, and the mules started up the steep hill. "Whadda you mean, I'll have him? Like a man like him would give me a second look."

A pair of lines appeared between Addy's eyes, and she pursed her lips as she examined Tuck. "It's true, you are a little rough looking, but only because of the way you dress and act."

"What's wrong with the way I dress and act?" Tuck felt the insult but wasn't about to let Addy know. "Just because I don't simper and primp?"

"Oh, never mind, sister. Let's not fight. The woods are so beautiful today. Let's enjoy the ride home."

Tuck relaxed and shifted a little on the seat. Addy was right. Oak trees, silver maple, and ash filled the woods on either side of the bumpy road, the sun glinting on their silver and green leaves. Soon the summer would be over, and gold, red, and orange would appear. Nothing was as beautiful as fall in the Ozarks. She grinned. Except maybe deep blue eyes and shiny black hair.

"So what did you mean about the way I look and act?" Tuck asked.

Addy huffed. "Really, Tuck, you're a very pretty girl if you'd let me fix you up like I'm always offering. Those braids are childish and make you look like a little girl, instead of a twenty-year-old woman. And when you're not wearing overalls, your dresses look disheveled. And. . .and. . .maybe you should use your first name."

"Well okay, maybe to the fixing up, but I'll never give up Kentucky." She gave Addy a sidewise glance. "You liked him, too. Why'd you change your mind?"

Addy laughed. "I hardly even know the man. I only met him at the store one day. I thought he was handsome. That was all. But he's the first one you've ever shown the slightest interest in, except maybe Rafe."

"Rafe?" Tuck laughed. "He's my best friend. You know that."

"Yes, but sometimes I've seen you two looking at each other with that. . .ummm. . .that look." She averted her eyes and stared at the woods.

"What look?" Tuck frowned, and indignation rose up like a cyclone inside her. "You better take that back. You know there's nothing between Rafe and me. And don't you go saying there is."

"All right, all right. Calm down. I must have been mistaken."

"I'll say you are." She gave a short laugh and flicked the reins. "Hiya. Let's go, mules."

꘎

Rafe chewed on a piece of green sour dock and watched as Tuck baited her hook, swung the line over the side of the boat, and then settled down on the bench seat.

She glanced at him. "Hey, aren't you gonna fish?"

"Naw, ain't in the mood." He chewed on the stalk and swallowed.

"Why'd you want to go fishing then?" She squinted. "You better quit chewing on that dock. The other day, I heard someone say it's poisonous."

Rafe stared at her. "You chew on the stuff all the time."

Tuck frowned then looked intently down at the water. "No, I don't. Not anymore. It ain't ladylike."

Rafe chuckled. "Ladylike? Since when do you care about that stuff?"

She checked her line then slung a glance his way. "Since a certain doctor moved to town. That's when."

Huh? Did she mean what it sounded like she meant? Rafe sat up. "What are you talking about?"

She bit her bottom lip, and her big blue eyes studied him for a moment. "Promise you won't tell anyone?"

"What do I look like? Some gossipy old woman?" He shrugged. "Tell me or not. It doesn't matter to me."

"Sorry. Guess I'm a little fidgety talking about it." She hesitated, and a blush washed over her face. "Truth is, I'm kind of sweet on the new doctor."

Rafe tensed and took a deep breath. He managed a sharp laugh. "I see. So is he sweet on you, too?"

"How should I know? I've never even spoken to the man." Her face softened, and tenderness filled her eyes. Something he'd only seen on Tuck when she was talking about a new baby calf or something. "But he will be. I'll see to that."

A bolt of unexplainable anger shot through him. "Oh really? And how do you mean to go about it?"

"Not sure yet." She closed her eyes and sighed. "He's just about the handsomest man I've ever laid eyes on, Rafe. Hair black as midnight and deep, stormy blue eyes."

"You mean like Lexie's?"

She glared and gave a scornful laugh. "Of course not. The doctor's hair and eyes don't look like a woman's."

"Okay. Don't get so riled up. I get it."

She sighed. "I'm going to marry him, Rafe."

Rafe's chest tightened and a knot formed in his throat. He wasn't sure why, but he'd better do something before he exploded. He took a long, slow breath and drawled, "I expect you'd better introduce yourself to him and make sure he's interested before you start planning the wedding. Besides, for all you know he may be a mad killer."

She gave him a shove, rocking the boat. "He is not, Rafe Collins. And stop making fun of me."

"Why, Tuck honey, I wouldn't think of making fun of you. Just want to make sure you're not murdered on your wedding night." He ducked, expecting a bucket full of bait in his face.

"Why you. . ."

Tuck stood, and the next thing Rafe knew he was treading water. He shook a wet cascade from his face and looked around. Several feet away, Tuck's head bobbed in the river and she grabbed for the boat. He swam over to help right it. Sputtering and gagging, they flipped it over and together dragged it to the riverbank.

Rafe hunched over, his hands on his knees and coughed up water. Glancing over to make sure Tuck was okay, he threw himself onto the wet ground, heaving deep breaths.

Loud, guffawing laughter exploded near his ear, and Rafe flipped over on his stomach. Tuck lay on her back, slapping her legs as she howled.

What did she think was so funny? "Tuck, you know better than to stand up in a boat, you idiot."

"Sorry. I got so mad I just stood right up, didn't I?" She grinned at him, her eyes sparkling. "Bet you didn't mean to go swimming today."

Try as he would, he couldn't keep a straight face. His

laughter joined hers, echoing across the valley.

Finally, she jumped up and started wringing out her shirt. His breath caught in his throat. The sun shone on her hair, giving it the appearance of gold threads. And droplets of water glistened on her skin. Rafe had never seen such a beautiful sight.

He shook his head. What in thunder was the matter with him? It was only Tuck. His best friend. The nutty tomboy who lived on the next farm.

He cleared his throat. "Look, Tuck. I'm sorry I teased you. But you aren't serious about marrying that doctor, are you?"

She stood with one boot in her hand and a faraway look crossed her face. "Dead serious. I've never been more serious about anything in my whole life."

two

Tuck jumped off her horse, Sweet Pea, and tied the reins to the rail in front of the general store. Her stomach tossed and turned, but that was good. Maybe that meant she really was sick, instead of just faking as she'd planned. She swallowed past a lump in her throat. On the other hand, this might not be such a great idea after all.

She glanced at the store then back to her horse, envisioning herself mounting Sweet Pea and riding away. She shook her head. Nope. She'd come this far; she wasn't about to back down now. Especially since she'd gone to the trouble of donning a freshly pressed dress with rickrack around the neck. She'd even wound her braids around her head. Taking a deep breath, she headed for the store.

The bell over the door jangled loudly as she walked in. She barely noticed the blended aromas of cinnamon and cloves, leather and coffee. Probably because her face, including her nose, was numb. She took a deep breath and stepped forward.

Mr. Hawkins looked up from where he was shelving buckets of sorghum. "Good morning, Tuck. What can I get for you?"

She cleared her throat. "Is the doctor here?"

Hawkins motioned toward a door in back near the post office. "Yes, his office is back there. He has a patient though."

Disappointment wrestled with relief. "Oh. Then I'll come back another time."

"No, don't leave. They should be about finished in there. Been near onto a half hour. Sit down there and wait." He motioned to a chair by the office door then scanned Tuck's face. "You sick?"

"Why else would I want to see the doc?" Her face prickled with heat.

He grinned. "Oh, maybe the same reason half the girls in the county been showing up here. Maybe you've taken a shine to the doctor?"

She opened her mouth to retort, but a choking sound was all that came out. Whirling, she stomped toward the door.

"Now hold on, Tuck. Don't get so riled up. I was just fooling."

Tuck stopped in her tracks, torn between escape from embarrassment and her desire to see the doctor. She'd made several attempts to get his attention, but aside from being polite, he had practically ignored her.

The door to the office opened and a woman came out leading a small boy. She nodded at Tuck and Mr. Hawkins as she walked by.

Tuck's breath caught in her throat as the doctor appeared in the open doorway.

"You have another patient here, Dr. Fields." Mr. Hawkins motioned to Tuck.

Surprise crossed his face, but he smiled, his eyes quickly running down the length of her then back to focus on her face. "Ah, Miss Sullivan. I didn't expect you back again so soon."

Oh no. She was blushing again. But what did he mean, again?

Mr. Hawkins cleared his throat. "Excuse me, Doc. This is Miss Abigail Sullivan. The young lady who was here yesterday was her twin sister, Adeline."

What? Addy was here? What was she up to?

"Of course," the doctor said. "I should have noticed. Please forgive me, Miss Sullivan. Won't you come in?"

Tuck nodded and followed him into his office, her head swimming.

A new desk stood against a back wall, the new wood smell wafting across the room. He motioned to the chair in front of it. "How may I assist you, Miss Sullivan?"

She ran her tongue across her dry lips. "I'm feeling a little bit under the weather." At least she could say it now without lying.

"I see." He smiled and his eyes seemed to bore into her. Could he possibly know she was faking? "What are your symptoms?"

"Uh. . .my head and stomach hurt, and I'm a little bit dizzy." That much was true. Even if it was nerves or lovesickness.

"I see." He reached down and took her hand, giving it a squeeze before he checked her pulse rate. He gazed into her eyes and smiled. "Yes, your pulse is a little fast."

Taking the stethoscope from around his neck, he bent over and listened to her heart. "Ummhmm." He moved the instrument to her back. "Take a deep breath now."

She hadn't realized she was holding her breath until then. She let the air out of her lungs with a *whoosh* then drew it back in.

The doctor stood. "I don't think it's anything to worry about, Miss Sullivan. Maybe something you ate. I'll give you some medicine to settle your stomach."

Was that amusement in his voice? Tuck gave him a quick glance, but his face was composed, except for that heart-melting smile, as he walked to a cupboard and withdrew a large bottle of pills. He put a few into an envelope and handed them to her.

"Thank you, Doctor." She stood and extended her hand to him.

"You're very welcome, Miss Sullivan." Tingling warmth

began at her fingertips and made its way up her arm as he took her hand and held it a moment longer than was necessary. "Is there anything else I can help you with?"

"Well, no—" She swallowed. "But did you know we're having a singing at the church Saturday night?"

"Yes, as a matter of fact, I did hear a thing or two about it." His eyes glittered as he looked at her.

"Uh, I thought, maybe, you being new and all, you might like to go along with me so I can introduce you to everyone." There. She'd said it. And hadn't even passed out.

"That would have been lovely, but you see, I've already arranged to attend the function with another young lady. Your sister."

Stunned, Tuck somehow managed to say good-bye and leave without passing out or screaming. Addy! So much for her sister's declaration about not caring for the doctor.

She mounted Sweet Pea and flung her knee around the horn. Last time she'd wear a dress on a horse. Wasn't anything wrong with her overalls anyway. Oh! That Addy. Just wait till she got a hold of her sister. She'd. . .she'd. . . Well, she wasn't sure, but Addy wasn't getting away with this.

Tuck set Sweet Pea into a thundering gallop down the road toward home, rushing past ancient, tall trees and herds of cattle as they raced toward home. Papa Jack would be madder than a wet hen if he saw how she was riding the horse, but who cared? He wasn't her pa anyway.

Shame shot through her, but she ignored it. It was true. He wasn't. Even if he and Lexie did raise her and Addy after their pa got killed. Okay, adopted them, too, so legally they were her parents, but so what? She was a grown-up. She'd do as she pleased. And the first thing she planned was to give that traitorous sister of hers a piece of her mind.

She found Addy in the kitchen peeling potatoes.

As Tuck stormed into the room, Addy looked up startled.

"Abby, what's wrong?" Worry crossed her face.

"What's wrong?" Tuck mocked her sister then yelled, "You know what's wrong. You lied to me about the doctor, then went behind my back and invited him to the singing."

Addy's face went white for a moment. Then with more spunk than Abby had ever seen from her, she stood, her lips pressed together. "Yes, I guess maybe I did fib a little. Because I knew how much you liked him." She bit her lip. "But I didn't invite him to the singing. He invited me."

Tuck gasped. "Why you little liar. You know you invited him."

"No, I didn't. I promise I didn't. " Her sudden burst of spunk gone, Addy dropped into the chair. "I'm sorry, Abby. When he asked me, I just said yes, without thinking."

"Sure, without thinking of me and your promise," Tuck yelled. She knew she was making a fool of herself but couldn't bring herself to stop.

Lexie rushed into the kitchen. "Girls. What in the world is all this bickering?"

"She's trying to steal my fellow, that's what," Tuck accused.

"I'm not either, and anyway, he's not your fellow," Addy said.

"He would be if you'd leave him alone." Tuck glared.

"That's enough, girls. Stop it, right now." Ma Lexie stood, hands on hips, her lips firm. "You can discuss this when you're calm. I won't have you fighting. The very idea. Sisters. And twins at that. Fighting over a man."

❧

"What in tarnation has you all riled up?" Rafe frowned at Tuck, then reached beneath a hen and retrieved an egg.

"I got a right to be riled up. Addy outright lied to me. Twice." She dropped an egg into the basket she carried then held the basket out to Rafe.

Rafe couldn't help but laugh as he dropped the egg into the basket. "I can't imagine Addy lying about anything. What are you talking about?"

"Of course you can't. Because she has you fooled just like everyone else." Tuck slung her fists against her hips, her eyes widening as she realized her mistake. The egg she'd just stolen from a Rhode Island Red mother-to-be had shattered, its contents running down the side of her overalls.

Rafe howled with laughter.

She glared at him then burst out laughing. "Guess I'd better be more careful."

"Yes, if you don't want to end up with egg all over you." He grinned. "Now what did Addy do to get you so mad?"

She grabbed a handkerchief from her pocket and tried to clean off the mess. "Like I said, she lied to me. Told me she didn't care anything about the doc. Then she went behind my back and got him to invite her to the singing."

"Oh." He hesitated. He'd planned to ask Tuck to go to the singing with him, but maybe this wasn't the time. "If he likes Addy, I don't see that's her fault."

"Thanks a lot, Rafe," Tuck snapped. "That makes me feel a lot better."

"I only meant—"

She waved her hand in his direction and he stopped. In silence, they finished gathering the eggs and took them to the kitchen, then went out on the back porch.

Rafe stumbled around in his mind for a good change of subject. "Let's go fishing, Tuck."

"Don't feel like fishing." She leaned against the house and moped.

"What? Since when did you ever not feel like fishing?"

"Since Addy stole my man."

Rafe's stomach knotted at the words. If he didn't know better, he'd think he was jealous. But that was just ridiculous. Tuck was his buddy. Had been since they were little tikes. Besides, she wasn't even pretty. Was she?

The thought of her the day they'd fallen into the river

invaded his mind. He sat on the step and took a long look. Blond twigs stuck out from the braids across her shoulders, and a few wisps curled around her forehead. Her blue eyes, dark with anger, sparkled as she glared at him. His palms went suddenly moist and his breath quickened.

"Why are you looking at me like that?" she asked.

Rafe came to himself with a start. How had he been looking at her? "I was just thinking about Addy," he lied.

"What about her?" A frown puckered the skin between her brows.

"Maybe it's time you give in and let her have something she wants for a change."

"What? She always gets her way." Surprise sounded in her voice and registered on her face.

"Tuck, no she doesn't. Addy gives in to you about everything. Maybe it's time you return the favor."

Tuck's mouth dropped open. "Well, I'll be. I thought you were my best friend, and here you go taking up for that—" He watched her storm into the house, slamming the screen door behind her.

Rafe sighed. He'd handled that well. As he turned away, he spotted Miz Lexie heading to the clothesline, a basket in her arms. An idea formed in his mind. He crossed the yard and took the heavy basket of wet clothes. "Let me carry this for you, ma'am."

"Thank you, Rafe. But you didn't really have to do that."

"It's okay." He set the basket on the ground by the clothesline pole. He grabbed a towel and handed it to her.

She gave him a curious look. "You and Abby fighting?"

"Sort of. She's mad because I took up for Addy."

"I see. . ." She seemed to be waiting.

Rafe cleared his throat. "Do you think she's serious about this doctor fellow?"

"Who? Addy?"

"No, I mean Tuck."

Understanding crossed her face. She placed her hand on Rafe's arm and smiled. "I wouldn't worry about it, Rafe. She hardly knows the man."

"Oh, I'm not worried. Just wondering. I mean, why should I worry? Tuck and me, we're just—" At the doubtful look on her face, he took a breath and blew it out. "This is crazy, but I think I might be falling in love with Tuck."

Lexie threw one end of a sheet over the line, motioning for Rafe to take the other end. "Have you told her?"

"No, ma'am." The horror in his voice was an exact match for what he felt. "She'd probably hit me with a hammer if I told her that."

A peal of laughter rippled from Lexie's throat. "Don't be too sure of that, Rafe. You and Abby have been very good friends for a lot of years. And that's nothing to scoff at."

"You think I have a chance against this doctor?"

"What do you think?"

He thought for a minute. The new man in town didn't know Tuck. Not like Rafe did.

"You're right. I'm not giving her up without a fight."

"Good for you." Lexie grinned. "Now how about helping me with the rest of these heavy sheets?"

three

Tuck jerked awake and sat bolt upright. What had woken her? She glanced around. Moonlight streamed in through the window and washed a narrow swath halfway across the floor.

A muffled sob came from Addy's side of the bed.

Tuck caught her breath as guilt stabbed her conscience. She'd said some pretty mean things to Addy after they went to bed. Whispered them to her in the darkness, so Ma wouldn't hear. But surely that wouldn't cause Addy to cry like that. Shucks, if it had been the other way around and her sister had talked to her that way, she would've been mad, not sad. Still, the guilt gnawed at her. Addy wasn't like her.

She leaned back on one elbow and placed her hand on Addy's shoulder.

Addy flopped over onto her back. Tears streamed down her cheeks, and her eyes were red. She must have been crying for a long time.

"I'm so sorry I agreed to go to the singing with Dr. Fields." Her voice quivered and heart-wrenching sobs interspersed her words. "It just happened so fast, I said yes without even thinking about how much you liked him." Addy paused and blew her nose on the sodden hankie in her hand. "I'll go right into town tomorrow and tell him I've changed my mind. Will you forgive me? Please?"

Tuck stared at her twin, and shame began to work its way into her heart. She had known from the start Addy liked the doctor, regardless of her declaration to the contrary. Maybe Rafe was right.

She opened her mouth to speak and then clamped it shut. Why should she let Addy have the doc? She swallowed past the lump in her throat and managed to form a sincere expression on her face. "Are you sure, Addy? I mean. . .if you really like him—"

"Oh no, I don't like him at all. I've no idea why I agreed to go with him. But please tell me you don't hate me. I can't stand it when you're angry with me."

"Of course I don't hate you, silly." Tuck licked her lips as her conscience stabbed her again. "We're sisters, aren't we?"

Addy flung her arms around Tuck's neck and hugged her tightly. "I'm so glad you feel that way, too. Ma was right. We shouldn't let anything or anyone come between us." She jumped out of bed and padded across the floor.

The sound of a drawer sliding open was followed by a *thud* as it closed. After a scamper, her sister climbed back into bed and placed something hard into Tuck's hand. "I want you to have this."

Tuck opened her hand and made out the gold heart-shaped locket that held tiny photos of their real father and mother. When she'd claimed their grandfather's violin, a family heirloom brought all the way from Ireland, she and her sister had agreed that Addy should have their mother's locket.

Tuck shoved the necklace toward her sister. "No, it's yours. I have the fiddle. That's what we decided."

"I know, but I want you to have it. Really, I do." Her tear-filled blue eyes almost pleaded.

"Well, okay, if that's what you want." Tuck frowned. "Are you sure?"

"Yes, yes! Put it on." The eager words, a little too cheerful, rang in Tuck's ear. Addy grabbed the locket and placed the chain around her neck. "Here. Let me fasten it for you."

The chain, cold to Tuck's skin, nevertheless seemed to sear

it. She shivered. Reaching up, she tucked it under the collar of her nightgown.

"There, now all is well again." Addy smiled and threw her arms around Tuck.

She accepted the hug, patting her sister on the back, stifling a sigh. A hound's ears couldn't hang any lower than she felt at that moment. Rafe *had* been right. Addy was giving up something she loved for Tuck. And Tuck was letting her.

She tossed and turned throughout the night, getting very little sleep. Between the rain that had begun in the middle of the night and her own guilt, her eyes remained wide and sleep eluded her. She'd promised to meet the oldsters for practice, so frustration clutched at her with every turn on the bed.

When she got up relief washed over her that the rain had stopped. But the still overcast skies didn't do much to improve her mood. She did her best to smile sweetly at Addy during breakfast, although every time her sister looked her way, her heart felt like it would explode right up out of her throat.

After helping with the dishes, she waved a quick good-bye, and with instructions from Ma to stop at Branson's for thread, she rode to town.

Mud splattered on her overalls as Sweet Pea's hooves sloshed down the street. She was late for practice. And she didn't want to get griped at by the oldsters. The three old friends had met in front of Branson's store every week for years. In fact, that's where they were still getting together to play their music when Mr. Willie took her under his wing. The other two hadn't been thrilled about having an eight-year-old girl in their midst, but soon they declared she fit right in.

Branson's was too busy for them now though. It was hard to even hear their own music with people trudging in and out of the store so much. The young'uns screaming at the top of their lungs didn't help either. A couple of years ago, the four of them moved to the feed store down by the mill.

Maybe they'd be at the store waiting for her today, maybe not. The rain had stopped, but the clouds hung low and dark. Mr. Willie lived a good way down the river, so he might not want to chance it.

The feed store came into sight and Tuck grinned, waving at the oldsters as she pulled up in front.

"Hey, there you are." Mr. Willie grinned. "We weren't sure you were coming."

"You didn't think a little rain would keep me away, did you?" Tuck said, swinging her leg over the saddle and sliding off Sweet Pea.

"Naw," said Squeezebox. He cut a glance at Mr. Tom and Mr. Willie. A big grin split his face. "But we weren't sure if you might be spending time with the doc."

Tuck scowled. "You don't need to worry about that. I don't think he even knows I'm around."

Mr. Tom coughed. "Okay, we need to get going here. Get tuned up, Tuck."

The music practice went well, until Mr. Willie took offense at Tuck's attempt at an unplanned solo. "What in thunder do you think you're doing, going off on yore own like that? You trying to be some kind of queen bee or something?" The old man shoved his hat back and glared.

"Sorry." She knew she shouldn't have done it, but sometimes she couldn't help herself. Anyway, he didn't have to be mean about it. "Don't get so riled up. What's wrong with being a little creative?"

"Oh, so that's what you call it. How about lettin' the rest of us know next time you feel like getting creative." He stomped off without another word.

The rest of the group broke up, agreeing to meet the

following week, and Tuck put her fiddle in the case and headed toward Branson's to pick up Lexie's thread before she headed out of town.

A rider on a bay mare came into view. Her breath caught in her throat. Sam Fields. And here she was in mud-spattered overalls and pigtails.

She straightened her back and forced a smile as he approached.

He tipped his hat then was past her without even a howdy-do. The very idea. . .how rude was that? He could have at least returned her smile.

She groaned. What did she expect, the way she looked. Why hadn't she worn something pretty and fixed herself up a little? She snorted. Because it was a muddy day, that was why. Mr. Stuck-up could just go butt his head against a stump for all she cared.

Sure. She didn't care. Not much, she didn't.

She sighed. As much as she hated to turn to Addy for another favor, it was time to come up with a plan to win the doc. Because she would win him, one way or another.

❧

Tuck sat on a stool at the back of the stage with the oldsters and tuned her fiddle.

Horace Packard stood at the podium rifling through the songbook. His brothers joined him and began tuning their guitars. The Packard brothers were well known in the area for their singing and guitar playing, but they didn't mind sharing the stage with Tuck and her friends.

Tuck scanned the audience, keeping track of the doctor. She grinned as she saw him slip into a chair in the third row behind Ma and Pa and Addy. He'd be able to see her new blue dress perfectly from there. Addy had told her it made her eyes a deep, romantic blue. Of course, she had the same color eyes, and Tuck hadn't noticed anything special about them when Addy wore this color.

She looked down at her fiddle then, unable to resist, chanced another glance at the doctor. Was he looking at her or staring at Addy? She took a deep breath and counted to ten. She wouldn't look again. Why should she waste her time on a man that only had eyes for her sister?

And why was that? They were almost identical. Addy had dressed her hair for her, so that soft curls framed her face, with the back pulled into something called a French twist. She'd put on a very pretty dress just for him. It wasn't very comfortable either. She ran her finger under the collar and tried to loosen it, then quickly dropped her hand as Addy frowned and shook her head.

After an hour of robust singing, the Packard quartet performed two special numbers. Then Tuck and her friends delighted the crowd with a lively rendition of "Old Joe Clark."

As the audience applauded, Horace stepped up front and clapped his hands to get attention. "All right, neighbors. I know you're all about as ready for a break as I am. The ladies have loaded the tables down with all kinds of sandwiches and desserts and other delicious foods. So let's enjoy it. Then we'll come back and sing a while longer."

Laughter and small talk exploded as everyone stood and began talking to their friends.

Tuck glanced around, searching for Sam. She spotted him just as he stepped outside. She managed to avoid her family as she wove her way through the crowd to the door. Maybe she could find a way to speak to the doc alone.

Lanterns hung on trees and rails, lighting the yard. Tuck walked down the steps. Moisture clung to the brown grass and fallen leaves.

"You shouldn't be out here without a wrap, Miss Sullivan." The doctor stepped from beside the porch and smiled at her.

A ripple of pleasure coursed through her, and warmth spread across her face and neck. She bit her lip. Why must she blush every time he noticed her? "Thank you for your concern, Dr. Fields. But I'm not at all cold." That wasn't strictly true. She hoped he wouldn't see her shiver and catch her in a silly fib.

"Please call me Sam. It would please me very much." His eyes gleamed in the darkness, and she shivered again, but not from the cold.

"Very well. Sam." She'd been calling him Sam in her thoughts anyway. It was nice to have his permission. "Are you enjoying the music?" Oh dear. She hoped he wouldn't think she was fishing for compliments.

"Yes, I am." He grinned. "I especially enjoyed your part in it. You're very accomplished on the violin, or perhaps I should say fiddle."

"Thank you. Mr. Willie is the real expert. He taught me to play."

"He taught you very well." He spoke absently and glanced over her shoulder instead of in her eyes as he had before.

Tuck turned her head. Addy had stepped out onto the porch with a couple of their friends. Jealousy pinched at her. Obviously she hadn't much chance with Sam as long as her sister was around.

"I sincerely hope you enjoy the rest of the evening, Doctor. I must get inside." She whirled to go, wondering if he even saw her leave. As she passed her twin, she ignored her, pretending not to hear her when she spoke.

Tuck avoided looking in the doctor's direction the rest of the evening. And when the final song had been sung, she gathered her things and walked out to the wagon with Addy and their parents.

When she was seated in the back of the wagon, Ma turned to her with a smile. "You played beautifully tonight, Abigail."

She reached back and patted Tuck on the knee. "I especially enjoyed your solo of 'Standing on the Promises.' It sounded so sweet and pure with only the violin."

"Thank you, Ma. I played it for you. I know how much you love it." And besides, she'd felt guilty about the thoughts she'd had concerning Ma and Papa Jack lately. Knowing Ma had enjoyed her performance made her feel better.

"I sort of liked 'Old Joe Clark.'" Papa Jack grinned and clicked to the horses.

"Oh you would." Ma laughed then smiled as she touched his arm. Ma preferred the slow, sweet songs. She glanced at Addy. "You're awfully quiet, dear. Are you feeling all right?"

Addy darted a glance at Tuck then smiled at Ma. "I'm fine. Just a little tired from all the excitement."

Tuck cut a glance at her sister. Addy had no idea why she was angry. How could she? She hadn't done a thing but be her own lovely self. Tuck sighed. So maybe it was time to take some lessons from Addy, the irresistible one.

four

Tuck leaned against the counter in Branson's General Store and looked down at the notice in her hand. Mr. Hawkins had handed it to her with a grin the minute she and Addy had walked through the door. MUSICIANS WANTED. CONTACT WILLIAM LYNCH OR JIM CASTLE AT MARBLE CAVE OFFICE.

"Musicians wanted? Wahooo!" As excitement coursed through Tuck, she waved the paper almost under Mr. Hawkins's nose. "What's this all about?"

"Get it out of my face and I just might tell you." His grin softened the harsh tone of his voice.

"Sorry. Guess I got a little excited. But is this real? Are they planning some special tourist thing?"

Addy came running from the back of the store, her face pale. "Tuck, what's the matter? Did you get hurt?"

"No, no." She shoved the paper at her sister, never taking her widened eyes off the store manager. "Okay, now what's this all about?"

"That's the second time you asked me the same question." A teasing look crossed his face. "But I guess I won't keep you waiting. The Lynch sisters are going to Canada to visit family."

"Canada? How are they getting there?" Tuck couldn't even imagine how far Canada might be.

"Hmmm, I don't rightly know." He scratched behind his ear and frowned. "Train most likely. What difference does it make? The point is, they'll be gone for at least a month, maybe more. Lynch wants someone to take their place, entertaining tourists in the Cathedral Room while they're gone. I thought of you and Willie and the gang."

"A real paying job for us? Hot diggety." Tuck grabbed the notice from Addy who shot her an indignant look.

"Stop using slang, Abigail. It's vulgar and I don't like to hear it." Addy turned and headed back to finish her shopping but threw over her shoulder, "And Ma would be horrified."

"Well, don't tell her, sis. I got carried away." Tuck grinned and perused the notice again.

"Say, Mr. Hawkins. How long have you had this notice?"

"Since yesterday." He ran a cloth over the candy jar.

Tuck groaned, "They've probably hired someone by now."

"Don't worry. I stuck it under the counter. Didn't want anyone to beat you to it."

Tuck's mouth fell open and then exploded with laughter. "You're a true friend, Mr. Hawkins."

Fifteen minutes later, she and Addy headed out of town.

Tuck gave her sister a sideways glance. "I have to stop at the cave on the way home."

Addy grinned. "Like I didn't know that. All right. I'll wait in the wagon while you talk to them. Who is Jim Castle anyway?"

Tuck shrugged. "Never heard of him. Maybe a new guide or something."

Addy shivered. "I don't know how anyone can stand going down into those dark holes."

"Marble Cave isn't just a hole, silly. There are rooms down there. Do you think Miss Lynch would sit in a hole and play her piano?"

"Well, it looks like a big hole to me. And dirt everywhere. And there's no way I'd climb down from one hole to another like all those silly tourists." She stopped and gave Tuck a sideways smile. "Sorry. I know you like the place."

"That's okay. You never did care about caves and stalactites, even when we were children. But if I get a job here, you'll at least come hear me play, won't you?"

Addy bit her bottom lip. "Maybe, but I'll stand right inside the entrance."

Tuck planted her feet as the wagon rumbled and bumped down a hill. Exhilaration washed over her, and she grinned and snapped the reins. "Come on, mules. Faster."

She felt a tug on the back of her dress and looked over her shoulder to see Addy's white face.

"Mercy, Abigail. Will you please sit down before you fall off the wagon? Marble Cave isn't going anywhere."

Tuck huffed but plopped onto the seat. "I don't know why you're such a baby. Have you ever seen me fall off?"

"No, but you've come close a few times. Especially going downhill." Addy's voice was hoarse with fear and from yelling above the noise. "And I thought you were going to be more ladylike."

Tuck frowned at her sister. Why'd she have to be so picky anyway? "Land's sake, Addy. I'm wearing a dress on a weekday. What more do you want?"

"The question isn't what do I want. It's what do you want? You'll never attract Dr. Fields if you don't learn to behave like a woman instead of a backwoods mountaineer."

At mention of the doctor, Tuck's chest tightened. Her sister had a point. She pulled on the reins and the mules slowed down to their usual slow walk. "I don't think anything I do is going to matter. When you're around he doesn't even see me."

"Then make him see you." Addy's voice had softened. "You can do it."

Tuck shook her head. "I don't know how. It doesn't come natural to me as it does to you."

"You can learn how to be feminine. I learned by watching Ma. You were too busy hanging out with Papa Jack and your old mountaineers. Anyway, you weren't really interested."

Addy pressed her lips together and narrowed her eyes at Tuck.

"So. . .you think I can really make him like me?" Oh, that sounded pathetic. Like groveling. How humiliating. Maybe she should forget it and concentrate on her fiddling. But Sam Fields was about the best-looking man Tuck had ever seen and the first one that had bowled her over.

"I can't guarantee it of course. But if you learn how to be a lady, there's no reason he won't. After all, you're quite beautiful."

Tuck tossed a grin at Addy. "You just called yourself beautiful."

"Oh," Addy blushed and bit her lip. "I guess that did sound sort of conceited since we look alike. But I didn't mean it that way. I see you as you. Not as me."

Tuck knew what her twin meant. She, too, seldom thought about how identical they looked until someone mentioned it.

A little tug of excitement yanked at her stomach as they approached the hill that led up to the old mine. "Okay, hang on. If we don't pick up speed, we'll never get up this next hill." Once more she stood and flicked the reins. "Yee-haw!"

❧

Rafe stepped out of the cave entrance and wiped the dirt off his face with his bandana. He loosened his tool belt and carried it over to the shack that housed the office.

Jim Castle looked up from the desk he was bent over. "Howdy, Rafe. Platform all done?"

"Yes, snug as a bug up against the other one. Can't tell where one stops and the other starts. I'm sure glad Mr. Lynch decided to do it this way instead of moving that heavy piano to make room for the group."

Jim laughed. "Me, too. It would have taken at least four of us to move that monstrosity."

Since Rafe had begun doing some work on the cave, he

and Mr. Lynch's new assistant had quickly become friends, finding they had a lot in common. They both liked farming, fishing, and hunting. They were already planning to hunt for turkey on Saturday morning.

A knock drew their attention.

Rafe's mouth fell open as he saw Tuck in the doorway, with Addy behind her. "Hi. What are you two doing here? Come on in."

Jim jumped up, knocking his chair over. His face turned red as he scrambled to pick it up. Finally, he turned toward the girls, who stood staring at him. "Forgive my clumsiness. I'm Jim Castle, the assistant manager of Marble Cave. Is there something I can do to assist you?"

Rafe grinned at the amusement on both girls' faces.

Tuck stepped forward. "My name is Abigail Sullivan, and this is my sister, Adeline. I play the violin in a musical group and understand you have an opening for musicians."

Jim smiled past the surprised look on his face. "How many are there in the group and what instruments do you play?"

"There are four of us."

At the excitement in Tuck's voice, Rafe's heart went out to her. She'd waited a long time for an opportunity like this. She and the oldsters had been playing at social and church functions for years, but a paying position was special.

She continued. "Willie Van Schultz also plays the fiddle. Martin Tanner plays the accordion. He goes by the name Squeezebox. Tom Black is on the banjo."

Jim, who had been writing the information down, looked up and smiled. "And how can you be contacted?"

She gave him Mr. Willie's address and her own. "But the quickest way to get in touch is to leave word with Mr. Hawkins at the store."

"Thank you, Miss Sullivan. I'll pass this along to Mr. Lynch this afternoon. If he wants to interview you or have you come in for an audition, we'll be getting in touch."

Tuck grinned and offered her hand.

Jim shook it then held his out to Addy.

The girls left a few minutes later.

"You couldn't do better than to hire them," Rafe said. "They play at a lot of community things, and they're very popular. Willie and Tuck make magic on those fiddles."

"I guess you know the Sullivan girls pretty well." Jim looked down and peered at the sheet of paper on the desk.

Rafe chuckled. "I guess I do. We've been friends most of our lives."

"More than friends, maybe?" Was that more than curiosity in his voice?

Rafe shook his head, even though his friend wasn't looking. "I wish. I thought for a while we might be headed in that direction, but she's head over heels in love with someone else."

"Oh, is that right?" Disappointment tinged Jim's voice.

Rafe threw a quick glance at him. Was he interested in Tuck? But he'd only seen her this one time. Still, she was mighty pretty. Oh well. Neither of them stood a chance. She only had eyes for that new doctor.

After reminding Jim to meet him at the farm Saturday morning at the crack of dawn, Rafe mounted his dappled horse, Champ, and headed home. When he reached the turnoff to the Sullivan farm, he decided on impulse to go see what Tuck was up to. Maybe she'd want to go for a walk or something. After all, they were still friends, weren't they? And as far as he knew, she hadn't an inkling about his real feelings.

He found her seated on a stool in the parlor, with Addy behind her brushing her hair up and around some contraption.

"What's that thing you're putting in her hair? It looks like something alive."

Tuck twisted her head, and the contraption flew out and bounced on the floor. She squealed. "Now look what you did. What are you doing here?"

"What I. . . ? All I did was walk in the door." Rafe rescued the puffy brown thing from the floor and handed it to Addy. "Looks dead, whatever it is."

A giggle escaped from Addy's lips. "It does, rather, doesn't it? Better that than alive, I suppose."

Tuck snorted. "Don't encourage him, Addy. What do you want, Rafe?"

"I thought you might want to go for a walk or something, but I can see you're occupied with something more interesting, whatever it may be."

Tuck stood. "I don't feel like sitting still any longer, anyway. And fresh air sounds good to me. Let's go."

"But Abigail, I thought you wanted to try the new coiffure."

"Sure I do. But it doesn't have to be right now. Let's wait until tomorrow." She grabbed Rafe's hand and grinned. "Come on."

"Fine," Addy called after them. "I have other things I'd rather be doing, too."

Rafe laughed, suddenly lighthearted, and followed Tuck outside. Maybe she was coming to her senses.

They walked across the field toward the creek, hand-in-hand.

"What was that thing Addy was putting in your hair? It looked downright scary."

Tuck laughed. "It did, didn't it? It's called a transformation or something of the sort. You wrap your hair in it or around it or something."

Rafe glanced at her, puzzled. "But what's the purpose?"

"It's supposed to make your hair look about four times fuller, and you perch a hat on top. I think. It's the latest style."

"I guess this has something to do with the doctor?"

"Of course. He likes ladylike girls, so Addy's going to help me be one." She peered up at him, her blue eyes dancing.

"So you're going to pretend to be something you aren't, so he'll like you better?" Rafe's mouth suddenly tasted sour.

She jerked her hand away from his and glared. "There you go again. Making fun of me."

"I didn't mean to make fun of you, Tuck. It just seems to me, if a man doesn't like you for who you are, why would you want him anyway?"

She huffed. "You don't understand. Wait until you fall in love. Then you'll know why I'm trying to change."

"I like you the way you are, Tuck." He spoke quietly and wasn't sure at first if she heard him.

After a moment, she sighed. "I know you do, Rafe. But we're not kids anymore. Things change. People change. And I have to change."

"All right, Tuck. If that's what you want, then change. But stay yourself while you're doing it."

"Stay myself?" She laughed. "I'm not likely to be anyone else. I'm still me, Rafe. And we'll still be friends."

He stopped and took her hands, looking down into her eyes. "Promise?"

"Promise. Nothing will ever change our friendship, Rafe." She looked up and her eyes blinked back tears. "Only, you have to let me do this, Rafe. I really, really love the doc."

The words echoed in Rafe's mind as he rode home and dread squeezed at his heart. Was there any hope for him and Tuck? It didn't seem likely.

five

Huffing a sigh, Tuck lowered her fiddle again and pushed down on the top part of her sleeve in an attempt to flatten it.

A chorus of snickers sent a surge of embarrassment and anger through her. "What are you varmints cackling about?"

Tom coughed and guffawed. "Them sleeves look like legs of mutton, Tuck. Why'd you wear such a contraption to practice?"

"Laugh all you want to. Mr. Lynch said if he decides to hire us, I have to wear a fancy dress, so I'm trying it out."

"Sure you are." Squeezebox grinned. "Couldn't have a thing to do with the doc could it?"

"All right, that's enough. Leave her alone." Willie frowned at his friends and then nodded to Tuck. "Let's try again."

Tuck stood and placed her fiddle in the case. "It's no use, Mr. Willie. They're right. I can't play in these sleeves. I'll be back on Thursday."

"But what about the practice?" Tom whined and laid down his banjo. "I don't know that latest tune good enough."

"You can practice without me today," she snapped. "Mr. Willie, you'll have to play loud enough for both of us."

She turned, catching her hem on a nail sticking out from the wall. She stumbled before catching herself.

Tom and Squeezebox both burst out laughing.

Tuck reached down to loosen the fabric from the nail then glared at the two.

"Aw, we're jes' having some fun, Tuck. We don't mean nothing by it." Squeezebox grinned and nudged Tom.

"Yep. You're having fun all right. Fun at my expense. I'm

getting out of here. Bye, Mr. Willie." She stepped off the porch and turned the corner, heading down to the store where Addy and the wagon waited. She kicked at a piece of wood in front of her, flinging mud from the street, then continued on.

A horse whinnied loudly behind her. As she threw a glance over her shoulder, she felt her foot catch in the hem of her dress, but not in time to keep from tripping over the full ruffle. Arms and legs flailing, she slammed facedown in a mud hole.

"Abby!" Her sister's screams set her in motion, and she pushed herself partway up, then promptly lost her balance and landed on her seat. "Jiminy!" She squinted and shook her head, causing mud to fly from her hair and face.

The sound of horse's hooves and laughter preceded a familiar voice. "I do believe it's the lovely Miss Sullivan. Fancy seeing you down there."

Disbelief and horror shot through Tuck, and she peered up at the doctor's amused face. Oh no, she must look like a wet rat.

"It's quite rude of you to laugh at my sister. You are no gentleman, Doctor."

Tuck stared. Addy's countenance reminded her of a bear protecting her cub. Wow. Who would have thought Addy could be so fierce?

The amusement left the doctor's face and he dismounted, turning to Addy. "You are absolutely correct, and I apologize."

"I think you might be apologizing to the wrong person, Doctor," Addy retorted, tapping her foot on the ground. "My sister was the recipient of your untoward humor."

"You are absolutely right." Quickly, Sam turned and extended his hand to Tuck. "Please forgive me, Miss Abigail. I don't know what came over me."

Tuck accepted his assistance and the handkerchief he offered, scrambling up from the muddy street.

He placed his hand on her back to steady her. "I truly am sorry."

She peered into his eyes. Did her mean it? He seemed sincere.

Addy shoved him aside and, retrieving her own hanky, began to wipe the mud from Tuck's face. "The very idea of him laughing at you like that," she muttered.

The doctor cleared his throat, and Tuck glanced at him then quickly turned her face away.

"Well, ladies, if I can be of no further assistance, I'll be on my way." He remounted his horse, touched his hat, and rode off.

"I hated having him see me like this." Tuck gulped and blinked back frustrated tears. "C'mon, let's go home."

Addy trailed after her. "Really, Abigail. After his rude behavior, I don't know why you'd care what he thinks."

"Oh, he probably couldn't help laughing. I'm sure I looked very peculiar." She looked at her sister. "And he did apologize and was gentle and kind when he helped me up."

"I still say he was rude and ungentlemanly."

"And I say he didn't intend to be, so stop being mean, Addy." Tuck grabbed the reins from the hitching post and climbed up on the wagon seat.

"Very well." Addy climbed up beside her. "I'm sorry if I hurt your feelings. You're probably right."

"It doesn't matter anyway. Look what happened. I let you fix my hair, I wore a new dress—"

"And forgot to lift your skirt from the ground. Which is why you tripped." Addy smiled. "I think we need to work on deportment and carriage."

"Whatever you say, sis." Tuck raked back the muddy lock of hair that had fallen across her face. "I need all the help I can get."

"How did your practice go?"

"That's something else I need to talk to you about. The puff sleeves won't work when I'm playing the fiddle." Her voice sounded forlorn even to her. But no more so than she felt. "As a matter of fact, nothing seems to be working."

Sympathy crossed Addy's face. "It'll be okay, Abigail. You just wait. You'll have the doctor knocking on the door, begging for your attention. If you're sure that's what you really want. . ."

&

Tuck panted as she looked over her shoulder at her bulging derrière. "This isn't going to work, Addy. Aside from the fact I can hardly breathe, I have a shelf in front and a hump like a camel in back. Only lower."

Addy straightened from smoothing the dress down over Tuck's ankles. "Don't be silly. The special corset beneath your dress forms a silhouette called an S-bend. I believe it began in Europe several years ago and has been in fashion in New York City for a while now."

"So where did you get the contraption?" Tuck huffed. "And why don't you wear it yourself?"

"I sent off for it a few months ago but then decided I didn't want to stand out." She frowned and gave a little shake of her head. "The ladies around here dress more old style."

Tuck planted her hands on her hips and frowned at her sister. "Oh, but it's all right for me to be a laughingstock?"

"The doctor won't laugh." Addy grinned. "Who else matters?"

"How do you know he won't?" Tuck threw a suspicious glance at her twin. She wasn't absolutely certain she trusted her. Had she really stopped caring for the doctor?

Addy heaved a sigh. "Because, silly, he's from the city and is accustomed to the look."

Tuck puckered her forehead in thought. Addy had a point. And besides, she really didn't care what people thought.

&

Rafe dipped the huge turkey into near boiling water, being careful not to touch the side of the big, black iron pot.

He quickly pulled the bird out of the water and threw it, dripping onto the wooden plank where Jim was plucking the feathers from another bird. Rafe hunkered down across from him and started yanking feathers from the one he'd just dipped.

"Whew, wet feathers stink, don't they?" Jim said.

"Yes, but it's worth it to sit down to my ma's turkey dinner." Rafe grinned. "By the way, she told me to thank you for the turkey and to invite you to dinner after church Sunday. She'd have done it herself, but she had errands to run today."

"Tell her I gladly accept. And I was more than happy for her to take the turkey off my hands seeing as I'm living in a room at the Lynches' and they didn't want it."

They worked in silence for a few minutes, and then Jim cleared his throat. "How's Miss Sullivan? I haven't seen her in a while."

Rafe frowned and yanked a handful of feathers. "She's too busy turning herself into something she's not."

"What do you mean?" Jim asked.

Rafe sighed and stared down at the bird in his hands. "You see, she has always been so natural. Never putting on airs. A fellow knew where he stood with her and what she meant when she said something. Now she's turned into a simpering coquette. She's acting like a different person."

"Really? In what way?"

"Well, for one thing she never wears her overalls anymore. Not that I don't like to see her in dresses, but she's not being herself. That's the part I don't like. And she hasn't been fishing or hunting with me in weeks. Says it's not ladylike." He snorted. "Like she's ever cared. I feel like I've lost my best friend. Only worse."

Jim paused, confusion crossing his face. "Miss Sullivan wore overalls and fished and hunted?"

"Sure. Tuck and me have been fishing buddies since we were old enough to bait a hook."

"Huh?" Jim stared at him. "You mean Miss Abby is the one you're in love with?"

"Sure. Who did you think I meant?" Light dawned and Rafe chuckled. "You thought I meant Addy. Now I see. She's the one you like. I thought you had a hankering for Tuck."

"What a relief. That's wonderful." Jim threw his head back and laughed, and Rafe joined him, their laughter resounding through the yard.

"We'd better get these birds cleaned up or neither of us will have a turkey dinner, much less a lady." Jim laughed and focused on the feathers.

Rafe sighed. "At least you have a chance at the lady you're interested in. As far as I know Addy isn't seeing anyone."

"Thanks for that information. Of course, I'll be leaving as soon as the cave tourism stops, so I don't suppose it can go anywhere even if the lady should be willing."

"You could always come back," Rafe said.

"Yes, I can. And will." Jim's face brightened. "Don't give up on Tuck. If, as you say, she's not behaving like herself, then maybe this infatuation with the doctor will pass."

"Maybe. I hope so. But I'm not counting on it." Rafe sighed and shook his head.

They finished plucking and cleaning the turkeys and hung them in the cellar.

While they were washing up, Jim said, "What time should I be here for supper?"

"Ma usually has it on the table at six. It's only three. I think I'll run into town and pick up some more work gloves."

"Good. We can ride together until my turnoff to the cave."

Rafe grinned. "You sure you want my great company, or do you want to find out everything I know about Addy?"

"Yes, that, too." Jim took the piece of sour dock Rafe

offered him and bit down on it. His face puckered and he spat it out. "What is this nasty stuff?"

Rafe laughed. "I think you have to acquire a taste for sour dock."

They rode toward town, waving good-bye when Jim turned off toward the Lynches'.

When Rafe came out of Branson's store a little later, he spotted Tuck walking in his direction. At least he was pretty sure it was Tuck. But the strange outfit she was wearing made his mouth hang open. He shoved his hat to the back of his head and stared. Her front was thrust out like a board, and the rear end. . .well, he averted his eyes and waved.

Apparently she didn't see him. No wonder, her eyes were glued to the man on the horse coming around the corner.

Rafe scowled. Sam Fields.

Rafe watched as the man tied his horse next to his. Then with a brief nod at Rafe, the doctor sauntered down the road to meet Tuck. He extended his arm, and she rested her hand on it and simpered into the man's eyes. Tuck didn't even see Rafe as she stepped into the store with the doctor.

So that was that. Rafe mounted his horse and rode out of town. He wished he could keep riding until the sight of Tuck and the doctor was out of his mind. Trouble was he'd likely ride a long way before that happened.

Maybe it was time to leave. He'd never given much thought to leaving the farm, but there was no law that said he had to stay. Pa could afford to hire a hand to take his place. And Rafe's sister Betty and her husband Robert would help. Maybe he could find something to do in Springfield or maybe he'd hire on with the railroad. Yes, he could do that. Of course he'd need to finish the work he'd agreed to do at Marble Cave. Then, he was gone. And Tuck could marry her fine doctor.

six

The slight pressure of the doctor's hand on her back guided Tuck to the back of the store. An unaccustomed weakness washed over her. Was this how love felt? If so, she wasn't sure she liked it.

As Sam reached to open the door to his office, a slight cough behind them caused Tuck to turn her head.

Mr. Hawkins stood with a frown on his face. "You feeling sick, Tuck?" Although the store manager's words were directed at her, his eyes pierced the doctor as he spoke.

Sam turned, switching his hand from Tuck's back to her elbow. "Miss Sullivan and I are going to have a cup of tea and visit for a while in my office."

"Think so? Mebbe you can forget the tea and do your visiting here in the store, or else take a walk down the street."

Warmth washed over Tuck's face. It hadn't occurred to her there was anything inappropriate about being in the doc's office alone with him. Slight dizziness rushed over her, and she grabbed Sam's arm to steady herself.

"Are you feeling unwell, Miss Abigail?" The doctor's voice rang with concern.

Tuck's heart raced. "I'm quite all right. Perhaps we should take Mr. Hawkins's suggestion and go for a walk. A breath of fresh air would be nice."

"Very well, if you like." Annoyance had replaced the concern as Sam darted an angry glance toward Mr. Hawkins and steered Tuck toward the front door.

They stepped out onto the street and headed toward the mill. The amazing greens of summer had turned to brown patches in the grass and brown falling leaves from the heat. Tuck would be glad when autumn made its appearance and the world grew beautiful again.

"I'm very happy we met today, Miss Abigail. I've been wanting an opportunity to apologize for my manners the day you fell."

"Please forget about that, Doctor. You've already apologized and I accepted your apology." Tuck's voice sounded weak to her own ears and her chest felt suddenly tight.

"I'm so happy to hear that. By the way, I enjoyed your violin playing very much the night of the singing."

"Yes, you said that, too." Her head was starting to hurt as his voice droned on.

"Perhaps you'll let me know when you are entertaining again."

Satisfaction ran through Tuck. Perhaps the doctor truly did admire her. "Yes, I can do that. Actually we may be filling in as entertainment for the tours at Marble Cave for a while."

"Is that a fact? You be sure and let me know, so that I can be there." He squeezed her elbow, but amusement sparkled in his eyes as he gazed down into hers.

Was he making fun of her?

But the next moment his eyes darkened and his glance moved to her lips.

She trembled. What was wrong with her? She swallowed past the lump in her throat. "Are you very fond of music?"

He smiled and nodded. "Oh yes, I've been to many concerts in New York and have attended many of the finest concert halls in Europe."

"Oh, I see." No wonder he'd appeared amused about her fiddle.

A grove of oak trees, branches almost bare, stood near the mill. The mill owner's wife and two children stood on the bank of the creek watching the mules turn the water wheel.

"The wheel is splashing water pretty badly." Sam said. "Perhaps we should continue our walk in the grove so that you don't get wet."

Too late. The heavy tug of Tuck's skirts reminded her she'd forgotten to lift them. They dragged the ground, heavy with water. Besides, the thought of water droplets splattering on her skin was welcome at the moment. What was wrong with her? Had a sudden illness assaulted her?

As Sam turned Tuck toward the grove, the world began to spin around her and she felt herself falling. Arms caught and lifted her, and then she was floating in darkness.

❧

Tuck awakened to a tugging at the back of her dress and blessed relief as her clothing loosened. Strong hands rolled her over onto her back.

She gasped, and air rushed into her lungs. What? A memory surfaced. She'd been walking with the doc and must have fainted. Surely he hadn't loosened her clothing.

Her eyes snapped open, and she sat up. A wave of nausea washed through her.

The mill owner's wife ran a damp cloth over her forehead. "Now, now, Miss Sullivan. You'd best lie back down on the cot just for a bit. That ridiculous corset was cutting your air off. You'll be fine in a moment."

"Where am I?" She glanced around at the unfamiliar room.

"The mill office. Dr. Fields brought you here, and I could see right away what the problem was." A puzzled look crossed her face. "You'd think a doctor would have thought of that."

Gratitude washed over Tuck as the kind, round-cheeked woman patted her. "Thank you, ma'am. I was getting dizzy and weak, but I didn't realize it was the corset."

"I'll bet you've never worn one before." She smiled.

"No, ma'am. And I won't ever again either." And she'd

thought the strange sensations had something to do with love.

"I'd think your sister would know better." The woman prattled on. "She seems very fashion smart to me."

"It's not Addy's fault. I kept telling her to tighten it more." As she confessed, she felt foolish at the memory and changed the subject. "Is the doctor still here?"

"No, he left you in my care, dear. You needed a woman's help anyway." A knowing smile appeared on her face. "Right?"

"Yes, of course," Tuck said. "And I do appreciate everything you did for me. You may have even saved my life."

"Oh, I don't think it would have come to that, especially when you had a doctor right there with you, but you never know." She shook her head. "Dr. Fields said to tell you he was sorry to leave you, but he had a medical emergency."

"What was the emergency?" Tuck forced herself to fight off the resentment that assailed her.

"I don't know, dear. That's all he said. But it must have been serious. He was in a mighty big hurry to leave." She reached her arm behind Tuck. "Let's sit you up now and see how you feel."

Tuck complied and swung her legs from the cot. "I'm fine now. I appreciate all your help. If you could help me get laced back up, I'd best be getting home before it gets dark."

After thanking the woman again and assuring her that she needed no help walking the short distance to her wagon, Tuck left.

She'd just reached her wagon when she heard her name called. Turning, she watched Mr. Willie limp toward her. It seemed to her that his limp was worse. But then, he must be getting pretty old. The thought bothered her, and she shoved it aside and grinned. "Hey, Mr. Willie. Hadn't you best be heading home before dark?"

"Don't worry about me, miss. How about yourself?" He frowned then smiled, glancing at her dress but not saying a word about it.

"You're right. You want to ride along with me for a while?"

"It'd be my pleasure, Tuck. Got some good news for you." He loosened the reins of his grizzled horse and lifted himself slowly into the saddle.

"I could use some good news." Tuck climbed into the wagon and flicked the reins, heading out of town with Mr. Willie riding along beside her.

"Mr. Lynch sent word we've got the job. But he wants a list of the songs we're planning so he can approve them." He shook his head. "Can you believe that?"

Tuck laughed. "Yes, I can. You can't really blame him, Mr. Willie. You and Squeezebox come up with some wild ones sometimes. Remember 'Way Down Upon the Bloody River?' He wants us to entertain the tourists, not scare them to death."

The old man cackled. "Aw, that was just us a funnin'. I see what you mean though. I guess maybe we'd better get together and make him a list, then practice a couple of hours. When can you meet us?"

"I'll be in front of the feed store tomorrow at ten o'clock. That okay?"

"That's fine with me. I'll tell the others. We'll be there."

The sun was low in the west as Tuck waved good-bye to Mr. Willie as she turned off the river road and he continued downriver.

Tuck's thoughts were a jumble. She tried to focus on the numbers they should do for the entertainment. She'd been waiting a long time for a chance like this, but her thoughts kept jumping to Sam Fields.

He was a puzzle to say the least. One day he ignored her, the next he laughed at her, then again he treated her as though she were precious to him. Perhaps it was the new attire. If so, she was glad he liked her more ladylike appearance. She'd keep the hair and the ruffles, but the S-bend had to go.

❧

"Abigail! What in the world have you done to your skirt?" Addy stared, mouth agape at the sodden fabric lying in a pile on the bedroom floor.

"The question is what did this stupid corset do to me?" Tuck retorted. "It nearly killed me. That's what."

"What do you mean?" Addy's eyes widened at her words.

Tuck proceeded to relate the happenings at the mill, embellishing the story as she went along. "I'll tell you this much. I'm not wearing it again." She nodded, shortly.

"Oh dear. I don't blame you. I'm sorry, Abby. I didn't realize what torture it would be. But that doesn't explain your skirts. Did you forget to hold them up again?"

Tuck chewed on her bottom lip while she thought. "Yes, I did forget. But I've come up with a solution."

"What's that?" Addy looked almost fearful as she waited.

Tuck hid a grin. "I'm thinking about making me some of those split skirts they wear riding."

"All right. They're fine. Better than those awful overalls. But what does that have to do with your skirts dragging the ground when you walk?"

"You misunderstand, dear sister. I plan to wear the split skirt all the time. They only come to the ankle, so I won't need to worry about them dragging the ground, will I?"

Tuck grinned as Addy's eyes widened in horror at the thought. "Oh, but Abigail. You can't wear a riding skirt on the street. Or anywhere. They're just for riding. It wouldn't be ladylike to. . ."

Tuck burst out laughing, bending at the waist and slapping her hands against her bare knee.

"Fine. Go ahead and make fun of me." Addy frowned then

smiled. "All right. I did fall for that one, didn't I?"

"Sorry, sis. I couldn't resist it." Tuck wiped her eyes then pulled on a clean pair of overalls. She still wasn't ready to give them up at home.

"But you will wear dresses and style your hair?" Addy coaxed.

"Yes, if you'll help me. You know I can't fix my hair right." The last time she'd attempted to, it stuck out all over and finally came tumbling down.

"You'll get used to it. But of course I'll help." Addy smiled.

"Oh, I almost forgot. We got the job at the cave. Start in two weeks." She couldn't prevent the pride that filled her voice.

"Oh, that's wonderful, Abby. I'm so happy for you and your friends." Addy clapped her hands and her face beamed. "We'll need to get busy and fix the sleeves on your dresses then."

Tuck paused in buttoning her overall straps and peered at her sister. Why was she so nice? No wonder the doc liked her best. But now he liked Tuck, too. He had been a perfect gentleman today. Treated her like a real lady. That is until he left her passed out at the mill. But if he had an emergency, he had to leave, didn't he? Yes, but did he really have an emergency? Or did he just dump her and leave her?

"What are you frowning about? I'd think you'd be happy after your walk with Dr. Fields. It sounds like he's quite interested in you now."

"Sure. I think he is. Maybe." But a niggling bit of doubt wormed its way into her thoughts, robbing her of her joy.

"Oh, of course he is." Addy picked up the wet dress from the floor and hung it on a hook. "We'll need to get this washed tomorrow, so it doesn't stain."

Tuck glanced at her sister. Yes, Rafe had been right. Addy did give in to her and she'd always done everything she could to help Tuck get what she wanted. Why hadn't she ever realized that before?

"You don't have to help wash it, sis. I can do it." Tuck laid her hand on Addy's shoulder. "Why do you do so much for me? I hardly do anything for you."

"Now don't be silly. I enjoy doing these little things for you because I love you." She reached over and kissed Tuck on the cheek. "And of course you do things for me. Now we'd better go and help Ma get supper on the table. She's the one who really does too much. For both of us."

They found Ma Lexie in the kitchen, removing fried chicken from the skillet.

Tuck took the fork from her, and Addy poured vegetables into the serving bowl.

"Go sit down in the parlor with Pa," Addy said.

"Yes," said Tuck. "We'll call you when supper is on the table."

As they finished preparing the meal and placed everything on the table, Tuck's heart ached with sorrow and guilt. *I'm sorry, Lord. I wanted so badly to change after my baptism, but I've gotten worse. I'll do better. I promise. I'll stop being so selfish. I'll even. . .*

She paused. She'd almost promised to give Sam up. But surely God wouldn't want her to do that, would He? After all, hadn't He brought them together?

seven

Tuck climbed the ladder and peeked out the cave entrance. A crowd had gathered, and Jim stood behind a wooden booth selling tickets.

Tuck squinted against the sunlight and peered around for Sam. Not spotting him anywhere, she carefully made her way back down the wood rungs and across the vast entry cavern Mr. Lynch had dubbed the Cathedral Room. Probably because his daughter's baby grand piano stood in splendor near the back of the room. Or maybe because the ceiling was so high.

She stepped onto the makeshift platform that extended the stage. You couldn't really tell visually there'd been an addition, but it wasn't as sturdy as the original. It didn't need to be. They'd probably tear it down once the sisters took over the entertainment again.

When Squeezebox had spotted the dainty chairs placed on the stage for their use, he'd snickered. "These don't look like they'd hold a kitten. Hope I don't go crashing down."

"They're stronger than they look," Rafe had assured him, just before he'd left to help Jim with crowd control.

Anyway, the men would be standing most of the time.

Tuck perched on the edge of her chair, remembering to drape her skirts around her legs for modesty's sake. Her sleeves were now fitted instead of puffed. Not as pretty, but much more sensible for playing the violin. Narrow lace adorned the neckline instead of a collar. This was Addy's idea to prevent Tuck from folding the collar inside the neckline.

Tuck was becoming used to wearing dresses more often—

and frilly ones at that. She'd never cared much about being pretty, but that was before she'd met Sam. He appeared to like her new look and demeanor, although that was mostly put on when he was around.

He'd escorted her to church the past two Sundays and taken her for drives in his carriage several times. On the last occasion, when they were on the way home, he'd grasped her hand. She'd felt uncomfortable and after a few moments managed to withdraw it from his fingers.

The men were tuning their instruments, so she bent down and took her fiddle from its case. She ran her bow across the strings and smiled, satisfied with the pure, clear sound.

Mr. Lynch came down the wooden ladder. "Jim will be bringing the first group down in one minute. You may begin now."

As instructed, the three men stood while Tuck remained seated. When the first group entered the room, strains of "I'll Take You Home Again, Kathleen" met the tourists' ears. Jim guided them around the room for a few minutes, pointing out the natural carvings and other things of interest. Afterwards, he led them through the opening into the next room of the cave.

Tuck knew from experience they'd soon hear squeals from some of the ladies as they reached the area that led in a more difficult downward path, some of the chambers accessible only by rope ladders. Most of the women would turn around and scuttle back to be entertained by the music while their men continued the tour.

Rafe stood to one side. He nodded and smiled when he caught her looking at him. He knew how much this opportunity meant to her.

She glanced toward the stairs, frowning over Sam's absence. He'd promised to be there. Perhaps he'd show up later, unless another emergency prevented him from coming at all. Her throat tightened. Sometimes she wasn't quite sure about Sam's commitment to their friendship. And Rafe's open animosity toward the doctor bothered her. Rafe was usually a good judge of character. But perhaps he was merely jealous that Tuck had a new friend. And friendship was all it was at this point.

When the first group returned, Tuck jumped to her feet. They struck up a lively rendition of "Ole Dan Tucker" as the tourists exited up the ladder.

The next group should be coming in at any moment. Mr. Willie passed around a canteen of cold water, and then they fell into another tune.

Sam came down the ladder and threw her a wave and a wink before he hurried to stand to one side. Relief coursed through her. There. He did care. She must learn to be more trusting.

She glanced at Rafe and noticed he had puckered his lips in a silent whistle. She knew that look. She really must speak to him about his attitude.

≈

Rafe's stomach coiled when Sam Fields sauntered in like he owned the place. What was it about the man that set his teeth on edge? Partly jealousy, sure. But something about the guy rubbed him the wrong way. Had been that way from the moment he laid eyes on him, even before he knew Tuck had fallen for the doctor.

It bothered Rafe that Tuck couldn't see it, too. She was the one who usually spotted a phony at first glance. Maybe the stars in her eyes were blinding her. Or maybe there wasn't really anything to see. If that was the case, Rafe should probably bow out and leave the situation to run whatever course it was meant to. As long as Tuck was happy and taken care of, he would deal with it.

After the second group of tourists came down from the

sinkhole entrance, Rafe slipped outside. He had to get away before he beat the tar out of Sam Fields or did something else that would cause a ruckus. He couldn't ruin Tuck's big day.

He took Champ off his tether and mounted. The reins slashed back and forth as Rafe urged the horse to a faster pace.

He was halfway home before he made a decision and changed his course, heading toward the Sullivan farm. Maybe Jack could help him make some sense of this crazy situation.

He found Tuck's pa pitching hay in the barn.

Jack looked down and waved as Rafe came through the door. "Thought you'd stay and ride home with Tuck." He gave Rafe a questioning look.

"Sam Fields is there. I expect she'll be going somewhere with him." He climbed up to the loft and grabbed a pitchfork.

Jack stared at him in silence for a minute. "What do you make of that?"

"It's not my place to say," he muttered. But he sure felt like saying a few things.

"Since when? You've always had your say about anything concerning Tuck." Jack tossed a forkful of hay into the corner. "I haven't seen much of the man, so I'd really be beholden if you'd give me your opinion."

Rafe hesitated. But he'd planned on talking to Jack anyway, so he might as well just blurt it all out. "I don't like him. I'm not for sure just why. But something's not right. Maybe he's hiding something. Or maybe I'm imagining it, and I just don't like him because Tuck does." He paused. "I don't trust him not to hurt her."

Jack pursed his lips and nodded. "Appreciate your honesty. I'll keep an eye on him. If I see any sign you're right, I'll send the man packing."

"I don't know, Jack." Rafe shook his head. "You know how stubborn Tuck can be. If you ran him off, she'd likely take off after him."

"Maybe. But I hope she's a little more levelheaded than that." He arched his eyebrows. "What are you planning?"

Rafe shook his head. "How do you always read my thoughts?"

"If I could read your thoughts, I wouldn't need to ask what you're planning." Jack grinned. "But I can tell by that look in your eyes you've got something on your mind."

Rafe took a deep breath and leaned on the pitchfork. "I've been thinking about going to Arkansas and getting a job with the railroad. They'll be starting to lay the tracks soon between Conway and here for the White River Line."

"Hmmm. What about the farm?"

"The crops are almost all in. And it won't take long to get everything ready for winter. Pa can get Jim Shelling to help out if needed. Betty and Robert'll help, too. They only have a small crop this year. " He clamped his teeth together and kicked a small pile of hay off the loft. "I can't stay around here and watch Tuck marry that man."

Jack stood silent for a moment. Rafe was thankful when he changed the subject. "Speaking of the railroad, I hear there's a fellow named Fullbright trying to buy up land. They say he represents the Missouri Pacific. You heard anything about it?"

Rafe looked up in surprise. "News to me. Why would they need more land? They have more than enough for the new line already."

Jack shrugged. "May just be a rumor. You know how folks are."

"Yes, I do." Rafe frowned. "I'd hate to see anyone sell out."

"I doubt there's anything to it. The fellow may simply want the land for himself."

"Maybe." Who cared anyway? All he cared about was Tuck. Would she marry that guy? Or worse still, would Sam

Fields play her false and break her heart? The thought was enough to drive Rafe crazy. He tossed the forkful of hay into the corner and leaned the pitchfork against the wall. "Guess I'd best be getting home."

"When do you figure you'll leave for Arkansas?"

"Not for a while. I reckon I'll see you at church on Sunday." He couldn't leave. Not until he knew Tuck was safe and happy. Or at least safe. He wasn't sure he could control the happiness.

❧

"Amen." The preacher's voice boomed throughout the church and reverberated from log wall to log wall.

Tuck fidgeted as she waited for her family to exit the pew so she could follow. She'd thought Reverend Talbot would never stop preaching. Sam was supposed to have gone home with her for Sunday dinner. But he hadn't shown up for church. She finally reached the front door and hurriedly shook hands with Brother and Sister Talbot then stepped into the yard and glanced around.

Ma Lexie walked up to her and placed her hand on her shoulder. She smiled and gave Tuck a questioning smile. "Dr. Fields isn't here, is he?"

"No," Tuck said then hastily added, "but I'm sure he has a good reason. Perhaps an emergency came up."

Unease nagged at her. Sam seemed to have a lot of emergencies. This wasn't the first time he'd missed the service after promising to meet her there.

Worry lines appeared between Ma Lexie's eyes. "He seems to miss services a lot, don't you think, dear?"

Although the same thought had just crossed Tuck's mind, resentment welled up inside her. "After all, Ma, he can't help it if someone gets sick."

"No, of course not. I didn't mean to imply anything bad about him." Nevertheless, the worry lines deepened.

Relief washed over Tuck as Sam drove up in his carriage. He would surely have a perfectly good excuse for being late. "There he is now."

Addy gasped and headed toward the wagon.

Now what had got stuck in her craw? She probably had her nose out of joint because Sam wasn't interested in her. A pang of remorse shot through her. Addy wasn't like that. She smiled as Sam ambled up to her.

His eyes flashed as he gazed at her. "I'm so sorry, Abigail. I received word that a family downriver was taken ill. There were several children, and I didn't want to take the chance of waiting."

"Oh my," Ma Lexie said. "Of course not. Was it anything serious?"

"Thank you for your concern, Mrs. Sullivan. Actually, it was a simple case of the sniffles. And only two of them were actually ill." He smiled at Ma then shifted his gaze back to Tuck. "May I drive you home?"

"Yes, of course." Butterflies tickled her stomach and she smiled back at him. "And don't forget you're having Sunday dinner with us."

"That's right. And we'd best get going." Papa Jack nodded at Sam. "Lexie has fried chicken warming in the oven, and I can't get there fast enough."

Tuck sat straight in the buggy seat, proud to be riding beside Sam. He was by far the most handsome man she knew and the most distinguished. She was quite sure even Reverend Talbot was not as cultured as Sam.

By the time Sam pulled up in front of the house, Tuck was glowing from her own thoughts. She almost floated into the house.

Soon they were all seated around the table enjoying Ma Lexie's wonderful fried chicken, mashed potatoes, gravy, and sweet peas. Tuck couldn't help but notice that although

Pa and Ma were polite enough they both seemed a little reserved with Sam. But perhaps it was because they didn't know him well.

Addy, on the other hand, while not openly rude was obviously distressed and spoke only when someone addressed her specifically. Occasionally, she'd dart a glance in Tuck's direction, but when Tuck threw her a questioning look, she quickly averted her eyes and focused on her meal. Now what in thunder was wrong with her? Tuck didn't know, but she intended to find out before the day was over. She hoped her sister wasn't still holding onto a secret attraction for Sam. Because it wasn't going to get her anywhere. He belonged to Tuck, and she intended to marry him one day.

She swallowed past a sudden lump in her throat. Was she sure she wanted to marry Sam? She glanced in his direction and met his eyes. He smiled slowly, and his eyes warmed her as they seemed to send her a secret message. Heat washed over her entire body. Yes, of course she wanted to marry him. He was everything she admired in a man.

eight

Wind whipped through the entrance of Marble Cave, swooping down the opening, picking up leaves that had been tracked in, and scattering them around the Cathedral Room.

Tuck shivered, wishing she had worn something warmer. A storm had blown in within the last half hour. Overcast skies threatened a downpour, and temperatures were dropping steadily. She shivered again. It was too cold for this early in October. Well, at least now she could stop fidgeting over giving up the entertainment when the Lynch sisters returned next week. Now that a cold spell had hit, Tuck wouldn't be surprised if this turned out to be the last tour before spring.

"Think we'd better go on home?" Squeezebox turned miserable eyes on Willie. "This feels like a norther coming in. I can't imagine anyone tourin' a cave when it's this cold. My fingers are turning blue. I'm goin' to git cold blains fer sure."

"You mean chilblains don't you?" Tom snickered.

"Naw, I mean cold blains," Squeezebox snapped, frowning at his friend. "I reckon I know what I mean."

"Aw, it don't matter," Mr. Willie motioned toward the opening into the next room. "We can't go anywhere until Mr. Lynch brings them folks back out and says we can go."

Tuck blew her warm breath onto her cold hands. The tourists were due to be back in fifteen minutes or so. Were they ever in for a shock.

A wailing sound drew her attention. The four of them stared toward the opening, and soon Tuck could see the light from one of the lanterns. Mr. Lynch stepped through the opening, his face like stone, followed by a weeping woman and most of the other tourists who'd followed Lynch and Jim Castle down earlier.

Tuck's stomach lurched. What could have happened? Had someone fallen?

The distraught woman, tears streaming down her cheeks, grabbed Mr. Lynch's arm. "How long will it take them to find him? Is there any danger?"

"Mrs. Harris, please calm yourself. I assure you, we will find your son." But although his voice was positive, the uncertainty in his eyes was unmistakable.

"But we called and called. Why didn't he answer?" Her high-pitched voice warned of shock.

Tuck stared, dread filling her mind. A lost child? Oh no. *Please, God.*

Mr. Lynch sent an imploring look in Tuck's direction. She stepped from the platform and walked over.

"Miss Sullivan, this is Mrs. Harris. Her young son Tommy wandered away from the group. Mr. Harris stayed behind to help Jim search for him." His eyes spoke the danger that his words didn't as they stared into Tuck's. "I need you to get Mrs. Harris a cool drink and stay with her while I gather a search party to help."

His voice was calm, but Tuck knew the danger the boy might be in. According to legend, the Osage Indians used to call the cave Devil's Den and were afraid to enter. But that was due to their superstitions. At least there were no hostile animals inside. The main danger would be if the boy tried to walk around in the darkness. There were drop-offs and crevices he could fall into.

Tuck breathed a silent prayer that the child would sit still until they found him. If they found him. Folks had been lost in the cave before. Or so the rumors went.

As Mr. Lynch hurried toward the ladder, Tuck guided the

frightened mother to a group of chairs standing near the front of the room. "Please be seated, Mrs. Harris, and try not to worry."

She was relieved to see Mr. Willie approaching with a tin cup of water. She thanked him and handed the cup to her charge.

Mrs. Harris stared vacantly at the water and then looked up at Tuck, her lips quivering. "He said I was too slow. He pulled away from me and ran up to be with his father. I thought he'd be all right. Wouldn't you think so?"

Tuck wondered if the man had even known his son had run to his side. She took the chair next to Mrs. Harris and laid her hand on hers. "Tell me about your little boy."

"Oh, Tommy is such a busy little bee. He doesn't stay still a moment. His Sunday school teacher says he's the liveliest five-year-old she's ever seen."

Five? Why would anyone take a five-year-old child into a dark cave with twists and turns and drop-offs? Even with lanterns. And why didn't the woman call out to her husband and let him know the boy had run ahead? Anger boiled in Tuck, and she took a deep breath to calm herself. Casting blame wouldn't do any good, and furthermore she didn't know all the details.

"Oh." An agonized cry tore itself from the woman's throat. "It's all my fault. I should have made him stay with me. Oh what have I done? My little boy. My sweet baby." Mrs. Harris jumped up and rushed back toward the cave. "I have to find him."

Tuck caught her and turned her gently around. "Mrs. Harris, you'll never find him in the dark. Look, you don't even have a lantern. The men will find him. Come sit back down."

"But, I—" She looked wildly around the room, swaying.

Tuck caught her just as she fell. She laid her gently on the floor and called to Mr. Willie. "See if there's someone outside with a wagon I can borrow."

"What are you planning to do with her?" Mr. Willie yelled as he half ran, half hobbled to do what she'd asked.

"I'm taking her to Ma." Ma would know what to do. She'd take care of Mrs. Harris and help her through this until Tommy was found. Tuck shuddered then, with resolve, pulled herself together. She leaned over the unconscious woman and patted her cheeks. Pulling a hanky from her skirt pocket, she dampened it in the untouched cup of water. As she patted the unresponsive woman with the damp cloth, all she received was a moan.

A man in overalls came down the ladder, followed by a huffing and puffing Mr. Willie. Within a few minutes Tuck had tied Sweet Pea to the back of the wagon and climbed up on the seat. The Good Samaritan farmer whose name was Warren Holmes, lifted the half-conscious woman off his shoulder and up onto the seat where she leaned against Tuck's shoulder. The chill in the air sent a shiver all through Tuck's body. At least it wasn't raining yet. Within minutes they were headed down the hill toward the Sullivan farm.

Before Mr. Holmes had come to a full stop, Tuck jumped down from the wagon. "Ma! Addy!" She reached the door just as it flew open and Ma and Addy ran out.

"What in the world is—?" Ma took one look and ran to show Mr. Holmes into the parlor. She motioned to the blue settee. "Lay her down here."

As her mother and sister gathered around the prostrate lady, Tuck told them what had happened, then rushed to her room and put on overalls and a warm sweater. She grabbed her coat from a nail in the closet and threw it over her arm, just in case someone needed it. She rushed back to the parlor. "I have to get back to the cave, Ma. There may be something I can do to help." Tuck fidgeted from one foot to another.

"All right." Ma had opened a bottle of smelling salts and held it beneath the woman's nose. "She seems to be coming to. We'll take care of her. Send us word as soon as you find the child."

"I'll not send word. I'll bring it myself." She kissed her mother on the cheek and grabbed Addy by the hand, pulling her with her through the door and onto the porch. "Sister, please pray for someone to find little Tommy. I'm so afraid for him."

Addy squeezed her hand. "Of course, Abby. Let's pray now."

They bowed their heads and Addy spoke quietly. "Our Father in heaven, You know all things and see all things. You know where little Tommy Harris is right now, Lord. We pray Your holy protection over him and pray that You will keep him from being afraid. Guide the men who are searching for him, and let them find him soon. In the name of Jesus. Amen."

Tuck blinked back tears. This was the closest she'd felt to her twin sister in a long time. How could she have been so mean to her? Addy never had a mean or cruel thought for anyone. Reaching out she grabbed Addy and hugged her tightly. "I love you, sis."

The joy in Addy's eyes and her warm smile were all the response Tuck needed.

She jumped on Sweet Pea and headed back to Marble Cave, her sister's prayer replaying in her mind. Surely everything would be all right.

❧

Rafe removed his hand carefully from the rock slab and found another handhold further down. He reached with his foot and felt solid ground. The only problem was it could have been a six-inch ledge or one of the wide rock corridors that weaved throughout the cave. "Hey! Sam! I think there's a level place down here, but I need light."

"Rafe, that you?" Jim Castle's voice rang out, reverberating from the sides of the cavern.

"Yes, it's me. Dr. Fields was supposed to be holding the lantern. Where did he go?"

"Hold on. I'm coming down." A rope fell from above and then Jim slid down, holding on with one hand while the other gripped a lantern. He held it downward, and Rafe could see a huge cavernous room below.

Rafe turned loose of the rock and landed on the hard ground.

Jim slid the rest of the way down the rope. "Okay, we're down," he yelled. "Send us another lantern and mark the spot."

The rope was raised and soon was lowered again, this time with a lantern tied to the end.

Jim steadied himself against the rock wall while Rafe untied the lantern.

"Now, what happened to Fields?" Rafe asked.

Jim made an explosive sound of exasperation. "The good doctor grew faint and had to be escorted out."

"What? He was fine a few minutes ago," Rafe said. "How'd he get sick that fast?"

"Claimed there wasn't enough air, but no one else seemed to be having any problem." A wry smile twisted Jim's lips. "Anyway, I've seen cowardice enough to know it when I see it."

"So a man had to leave the search to guide him out." Rafe blew out a huff of air and hesitated. After all, this was Tuck's beau they were talking about. "I guess we really shouldn't judge the man. Anyone can panic. Maybe he has trouble with tight spaces." But all he could think of was that little boy, lost and probably scared half to death. His nephew Bobby's face popped into his head, and he swallowed hard to hold back the rising nausea. *Lord, please help someone find Tommy soon.*

"Maybe. We're more than likely better off without him. I

sure wouldn't want to trust him with my life or limbs." He glanced to his right then his left. "Looks like we'll need to split up here."

Rafe lit the lamp and headed down the dark passageway. Water dripped from somewhere above. "Tommy," he called every minute or so. But no answering voice came back to him. No little boy's cry. Not even a whimper.

❧

Tuck rushed forward as Bert Smith climbed out of the cave and half dragged Sam up after him.

"Sam," she cried out. "Are you hurt?"

His face red, Sam shook his head. "Got lightheaded and couldn't breathe. Not enough air I guess."

Surprised, Tuck glanced at Bert. His lips were pressed tightly together. He shook his head. "There's plenty of air in there. Well, I gotta head back in. They need every hand they can get."

Without even thanking Bert, Sam grabbed Tuck's arm and pulled her toward a log that lay on the ground. He dropped onto it, motioning for her to sit beside him. "That fool doesn't know what he's talking about. I tell you there's not enough air when you go deep inside the cave."

Tuck licked her lips. She'd never heard anything about thin air in the cave. And Bert had seemed upset. Had Sam panicked due to fear? She bit her lip. Everyone experienced fear, but to leave the search for a child and, to top it all off, to take someone else away, too. . . Wasn't that a sign of downright cowardice? She cringed inwardly at the disloyal thought. Of course Sam wasn't a coward. After all, he didn't grow up around here and maybe he looked at things differently. Besides, who could say for sure there wasn't a pocket of thin air inside the cave?

She took his hand. "Would you like for me to get you some water?"

He looked down at her hand on his and smiled, possibly remembering the time he'd attempted to hold her hand and she pulled hers away.

Heat burned her face. She removed her hand and placed it on her lap.

He stood. "Thank you, no. I really need to go home in case someone needs me."

Stunned, she stood and faced him. "But Sam, what if the Harris boy needs you?"

An impatient sound burst from his lips. "It's very unlikely they'll find the boy. And if by some miracle they do and he's alive, someone will come for me, I'm sure." He walked away and mounted his horse.

Tuck wrapped her arms around her shoulders and watched in disbelief and dismay as Sam rode away. Finally, she turned and went back to the cave, climbing slowly down the rungs of the ladder.

nine

Rafe peered through the narrow passage. He held his lantern aloft and saw another fairly large room. The oil in his lantern was low and he'd need to head back soon. As much as he hated the thought, he wouldn't be able to help the boy if he was wandering around in the dark, getting lost himself.

He took a step forward and slipped. Suddenly he began to slide down a wide crevice of some sort. He only slid a short distance before landing. He found himself in a small cavern beside a narrow opening.

He heard a sound. Holding his breath, he listened. There it was again. Was that breathing? Could Tommy be in there?

He eyed the opening, mentally measuring if he could fit through there. Only one way to find out. He squeezed through the tight opening and stopped still, his heart thumping. On the floor, next to a large, natural throne-like structure, lay a small boy, his blond hair resting on one small hand. *Please let him be alive.* Rafe stepped quietly across the way and bent over the tiny form. He breathed a sigh of relief as the child rolled over and opened his eyes.

"You found me." A smile split the small face and the boy sat up. "Will you take me to my mother now?"

Rafe heard the quiver in his voice and felt tears behind his eyelids, but he didn't care. He'd never felt the emotions he felt now at the sight of this small boy. "I'll be happy to do that, Tommy. Can you stand?"

"Sure I can." Tommy grinned and jumped up. "Isn't this a fine room? That looks like a throne over there, but it's not. My father told me all about it before we came to Marble

Cave. It's a rock formation. There's a bunch of them. Father told me water and stuff formed all these thrones and posts and things, but Ma said God made them like this."

Rafe's eyes scanned the boy from his head to his feet. He appeared to be fine.

"You must be a very smart boy, Tommy, to remember all that."

"Uh-huh." He held his hand out to Rafe. "I'd like to go see my mother now."

Rafe swallowed past the lump in his throat. He took the small hand and started back the way he'd come, boosting Tommy upward then pulling himself up after him. When they reached the place where he'd separated from Jim, he placed two fingers in his mouth and gave a loud whistle. The signal the child was found.

❧

Tuck stared in admiration as Rafe handed the small boy to his father.

Tears rolled down the man's cheek. "How can I ever thank you?" Mr. Harris held his hand out and shook Rafe's.

"You don't need to thank me, sir. Any one of us could have found Tommy. I just happened to be the one at the right place."

Mr. Harris nodded and looked around at the men who had followed Rafe and Tommy into the Cathedral Room. "There are no words to express my gratitude."

Tuck gazed at Rafe, pride filling her heart. A lot of men would be taking the credit to themselves, but not Rafe. He was good through and through.

He turned and their eyes met. Tuck took a step forward, her heart racing, and then stopped at the memory of Sam's face as he'd crawled out of the cave. She blinked back sudden tears as shame washed over her. Why couldn't Sam be more like Rafe?

Through a blur, she saw Rafe coming toward her. She threw him a sad smile then turned and headed for the ladder.

"Tuck, wait. Where are you going?"

But she was halfway up to the exit. She climbed out the top and ran toward Sweet Pea, who nibbled at the browning grass around her tether. Mounting, she urged Sweet Pea into a gallop.

Halfway down the hill, Tuck heard hoofbeats. Glancing over her shoulder, she saw Champ racing after her with Rafe leaning forward in the saddle, his face tense with determination.

Tuck sighed. She might as well stop. Sweet Pea couldn't outrun Champ. She pulled slightly on the reins, and Sweet Pea slowed.

Rafe pulled up beside her. "What in the world are you doing, running off in such an all-fired hurry, Tuck Sullivan?" Rafe snapped, his voice fraught with impatience. "Is that any way to treat a friend?"

Tuck gnawed on her bottom lip and threw him an apologetic smile. "Sorry."

"Well, I guess you ought to be," he growled. "So where are you heading so fast?"

Tuck shrugged. "Home, I guess. I need to let Mrs. Harris know her son is found."

"Jim was going to take Mr. Harris and Tommy over to your place to get Mrs. Harris," Rafe said.

"Oh. All right, but I'd better get on home anyway." Any place to get away from Rafe's searching eyes. Sometimes she felt like he could read her mind.

Rafe tossed her a sideways grin. "I've got a better idea. We ain't been fishing in weeks. What do you say?"

"Are you crazy? It's getting colder by the minute, and look at those clouds. We're liable to have a gully washer any minute now."

"Oh?" His eyes danced, full of challenge. "When did that ever stop us?"

Tuck peered at her lifelong friend. There was no denying she missed him. Why not go fishing? At home, she'd just mope over Sam. Anyway, she was probably making a mountain out of a molehill and thinking the worst. She cocked her head and grinned. "Okay, but if we get drenched, Ma'll be beside herself, and I'll blame it all on you."

Rafe tossed his head back and laughed. "Sure, go ahead. She won't believe you anyway."

He was more than likely right about that. She and Rafe had gotten into so much mischief over the years. . . "Okay, but I'll need to use one of your poles. I don't think I can get past Ma with mine on a day like this." She shook her head.

"Why, Tuck. Scared of your ma, and you a grown-up woman?"

"Oh, be quiet. I'm not half as scared of my ma as you are of yours. Race you to your place." With a "hiya" and a slight kick to Sweet Pea's sides, she took off.

They reined in winded in front of Rafe's barn, and he went inside and retrieved his fishing poles and a coat. Then they dug up worms for bait.

Rafe's old boat was tied up by the river. In no time, they'd shoved it into the edge of the water and jumped in.

"I'm sure glad your ma didn't see us. She'd have a fit if she knew we were on the river with the wind picking up like this." Tuck baited her hook and threw the line over the side.

Rafe glanced up at the sky. "I don't think it's going to amount to anything."

"Huh! That's what you said the time we almost got swept downriver," Tuck retorted.

"We made it okay, didn't we?"

"Sure, because the Maxwell brothers jumped in and grabbed the boat." Tuck laughed.

Rafe roared with laughter. "Good thing those Maxwells are all big and hefty."

"Wow, Rafe. We couldn't have been more than eight or nine. Just little tykes." Tuck leaned back and sighed. "Do you ever wish you were a kid again?"

Rafe's eyes darkened with emotion. He started to speak then stopped.

Tuck sat up. "What's wrong, Rafe?"

He exhaled and shook his head. Then gave a short laugh. "Nothing. Just thinking, I guess. But no, I like us the way we are now."

Tuck nodded and started to lean back when she felt a tug on her line. With a whoop she yanked. She grabbed the big mudcat and threw it into the bottom of the boat. "Ha, you're slipping. I got the first one."

"Yes, I see you did. Enjoy it. It's probably the last one you'll pull in. I, on the other hand, plan to catch a whole passel of them."

The first part of his prophecy came true, but to their chagrin, Tuck's mudcat was the only one either of them got. Too cold more than likely.

"Oh well. At least you were right about the storm," Tuck said as they moored the boat. "You know, this catfish would be mighty good cooked over an open fire."

"Well, I'll be. I believe you're finally right about something, Tuck. Let's cook it and eat it right here."

They made short work of cleaning the fish then cut it in half. As they sat holding their sticks over the campfire, the tantalizing aroma caused Tuck's stomach to rumble with hunger. After they'd eaten, she leaned back on her elbows, looking up at the clear sky.

The familiar camaraderie she shared with Rafe was like a warm blanket. Relaxation washed over her, and she realized she'd been tense all day. Maybe longer. Realization hit her. If she married Sam, she'd have to give up her friendship with Rafe. Sam would never stand for it. Unease prickled her skin and she shivered. Could she give up Rafe? The very thought caused an emptiness inside her.

But she loved Sam. Didn't she? A memory of his smoldering eyes burned her flesh, and excitement rushed through her. Yes, of course she loved him. And she wouldn't give him up.

≥

Tuck ran her finger around the rim of the pan then placed it in her mouth, tasting the sweet and sour tang of the gooseberry pie filling.

Ma Lexie smiled and wagged her finger. Tuck grinned. Ma was a good sport. Always had been, since the first day she'd taken two ornery little girls into her home. It couldn't have been easy for her, caring for eight-year-old twins with minds of their own. Not that Addy gave her much trouble, but Tuck knew she herself had been a handful.

"Really, Abby, why do you do that?" With a toss of her head, her sister grabbed the pan and scraped the clinging gel-like substance into the slop bucket, then put the pan into the dishwater.

"Oh, don't pretend you never sneak a lick, Miss Priss." Tuck snapped a dishcloth at her sister's retreating back, and Addy threw her a grin then stuck her tongue out.

Ma opened the door in the front of the stove and placed the pie inside. She wiped her hands on the dish towel Tuck had proffered and smiled. "Is Sam coming to supper, dear?"

Tuck frowned and shook her head. "He had a political meeting in Forsyth. I don't know when he'll be back. Tomorrow I guess."

"He's away an awful lot, isn't he?" Addy blurted then bit her lip.

"What's that supposed to mean?" Tuck felt anger soaring

up from somewhere deep inside. "He's a busy man with his medical practice, and he's involved in a lot of political stuff. What's wrong with that?"

"Nothing." Addy turned back to the dishpan. "I was just asking. Sorry."

Tuck grabbed a clean dishcloth and started drying the dishes. "Okay. Sorry I snapped. To be honest, I'm a little put off that he's gone so much. But I know he's a very busy man."

"Of course he is." Ma Lexie took a small pot off the hook and some potatoes out of the bin. With a sigh she sat at the table and started to peel the small brown globes.

Addy tossed the dishwater out the back door and wiped the pan. "Here, Ma. Let me do that for you."

"Oh no. It feels good to be off my feet for a while." She smiled and patted a chair. "Sit down. You, too, Abigail. I have something to tell you."

Dread clutched at Tuck. Ma had looked a little peaked lately. What would she do if something happened to Ma? She stared at the woman who had raised her as her own child.

"Is something wrong, Ma? You're not ill, are you?" Leave it to Addy to voice what Tuck was feeling.

Tuck leaned forward, her eyes glued to Ma.

Ma gave a little laugh. "Heavens, no. I couldn't be better. I have good news, not bad."

Impatient now that her fear was absolved, Tuck waited.

"You girls are going to have a brother or sister soon." Pink washed over Ma's face. And something else. Joy. That was it. But surely she didn't mean. . . Ma was nearly forty and had never had a child. Tuck had just assumed she never would.

"Do you mean—?" Addy had a grin from ear to ear.

Ma nodded.

"When, Ma?" The joy had somehow jumped onto Tuck as well, and excitement welled up inside her.

"The early part of March, I believe." So that was the reason Ma's clothes were looking a little tighter. She must be around four months along.

Addy jumped up and threw her arms around Ma. "What does Pa think about it? I'll bet he's hoping for a boy."

Ma laughed, a tinkling little joyful sound that rippled across the air. "He says he doesn't care, but I think he's secretly hoping for a son."

"Who can blame him?" Tuck grinned. "After being surrounded by females all these years."

"Blame me for what?" Papa Jack stepped into the room and planted a kiss on Ma's cheek, a lock of hair falling across his forehead. Sandy colored hair without a speck of gray. "Ummm. Is that gooseberry pie I smell?"

"Yes." Ma's eyes sparkled. "And don't you go getting any ideas. It's for after supper."

"Shucks." Pa shook his head. "But I reckon I can wait."

Tuck watched her parents. It was obvious to anyone they were still very much in love. Pa was always so tender with Ma, even while being playful.

Tuck sighed. Would Sam ever look that way at her? Would he ever touch her softly on the cheek the way Pa was touching Ma. She swallowed past the lump in her throat. Would she ever have with Sam the deep devoted love Pa and Ma had together?

ten

How in the world had she let herself get roped into this? Tuck shoved a stack of baskets aside and kicked at a tied-up bunch of cornstalks. "I don't know why people just bring things and dump them off. It wouldn't hurt them to stay and help."

"Now Abby, don't be like that," Addy said. "You enjoy the harvest festival as much as anyone. No one forced you to volunteer."

"Maybe they didn't force me, but I sure feel like I've been hornswoggled into it." She snorted. "Do we have to spend every spare minute we have in this place?"

"We do if we want to get everything done. And don't act like no one else is helping." She motioned to several women who scurried around sweeping straw from the floor of the Jenkinses' old barn. Since they'd built a new one, the old barn was used pretty much to store anything and everything. And of course to hold community parties and such.

"Who'd believe we had a dance here in the spring." Tuck shook her head. "Maybe they should do some barn cleaning in between times."

"Abby!"

At the distress in her sister's voice, Tuck looked up and caught sight of Mrs. Jenkins standing just inside the door. She couldn't tell if the kind woman had heard her or not. Why couldn't she learn to keep her lips buttoned up? She whirled around and lined a basket with straw, then placed small pumpkins inside.

Addy leaned over. "I don't think she heard you," she whispered.

Tuck sighed with relief. "I didn't mean it. I don't know why I blurt things out like that."

"Remember that time you called Mrs. Batson an old sow, and she overheard you?" A giggle rippled from Addy's throat.

"Yes, and the seat of my pants remembers, too. That had to be the hardest spanking Pa ever gave me." Tuck recalled the pain only too well, and she had to restrain herself from reaching back to rub her backside.

Addy giggled. "If you'd called her an old bear you'd have been closer to the truth. I never saw anyone so grumpy."

Tuck grinned. "She was grumpy. But I guess I gave her good reason to be."

"Yes, you did," Addy said, grinning. "Many good reasons."

"Sam was supposed to help today, but at the last minute he had to go to Forsyth on business." Tuck bit her lip and frowned. He seemed to have a lot of business lately. He was always going somewhere.

"Hmmm." Addy ducked her head and focused intently on an engraved walking stick that someone had dropped off for the festival.

"What's that supposed to mean?" Addy hadn't said two words to Sam lately, and it wasn't like her to be that rude.

"Nothing. Nothing at all." Addy glanced around. "I think I need to help them get those corn shocks up. They seem to be having trouble getting them to stand."

Tuck watched her sister scurry away. Addy wasn't fooling her a bit. She had something against Sam, and Tuck meant to find out what. Surely she wasn't still upset because Sam had chosen Tuck over her. She shrugged and got back to work.

"Abigail, what a pretty dress." Anne Lofting, a seventeen-year-old who thought she was God's gift to the male population, smiled at her. But the smile looked more like a smirk to Tuck. Anne had made fun of her more than once.

Maybe she was being overly suspicious and Anne really was sincere this time. After all, Tuck had thought Sam would be here, so she'd taken extra care with her hair and dress today. She knew she looked nice. "Thank you. They say blue is my color."

"Oh definitely." Anne giggled and sauntered away.

Tuck shook her head and continued filling a basket with apples and oranges, the aroma tantalizing her nose. The festival was only a couple of weeks away. She and the oldsters would be playing for the crowd. Their first time to play in public since the Lynch sisters got back last week.

There was a loud gasp behind her and she whirled around. Her twin stared at her with wide eyes, her hand over her mouth. "Abby," she choked out, rushing forward.

"What's wrong?"

"Turn around," Addy whispered through her teeth.

Tuck did as instructed and felt a tugging at her back.

"Your dress was tucked up. You must have caught it on something. Your bloomers were showing."

"Oh." Tuck blushed. "Must have happened when I went to the necessary earlier."

"You really must be more careful, Abigail."

"Oh, don't get your drawers twisted. Nobody saw them but Anne Lofting." But Tuck inwardly seethed. Her bloomers were pale blue.

"Abby! Don't you care that she probably told everyone?"

Addy's scandalized whisper tickled Tuck's ear and she grinned. "Nope, not a bit." That wasn't strictly true, but Addy was such a prude, it was fun to shake her up sometimes.

Addy clicked her tongue. "We need to finish up what we're doing and leave. Ma will be expecting us home soon."

Tuck glanced around. Baskets and tables stood neatly against the walls. Festoons of autumn colors were draped across the rafters and over tables. All they'd need to do was set up food tables the day of the festival. Then toward the close of the day, everything would go back against the walls to make room for the auction. Hal Swanson was the best auctioneer in three counties. Tuck could almost hear the rhythm of his voice and words now.

"Why, Abby, your face is flushed and you look so excited." Addy's eyes twinkled. "Are you looking forward to the festival?"

"I am excited. It'll be fun to have a party again." And to stroll around outside on Sam's arm, watching the shooting gallery and the ring toss. Or maybe she'd even allow him to hold her hand. She hoped he wouldn't have something to do at the last minute to prevent his coming to the shindig.

≈

Rafe stood beside the wagon and waited for his mother to come out of the Jenkinses' barn. His breath caught as Addy stepped out followed by Tuck. When she saw him she waved, said something to Addy, and then headed his way. His heart thumped so loudly he could almost hear it. He sure hoped she couldn't.

"Hi there, Rafe. Haven't seen you in a couple of weeks." She gave him an accusing glance.

Now why would she accuse him? "Not my fault. Every time I go to your place, you're off somewhere with Sam Fields." He hadn't seen her except at church since the day they'd gone fishing. He'd been hopeful after the good time they'd had together, but the very next day, he'd seen her making simpering eyes at the doctor.

"Well, after all, Rafe, he's practically my fiancé." She turned her head, and a hank of kinky blond hair escaped from the bone pin holding it in a knot at the back of her neck.

"Practically?" That sounded hopeful. "So, is he or isn't he?"

"He hasn't actually asked me yet." She tossed her head. "Not that it's any of your business."

He slumped against the wagon as she stomped off after her sister. He'd done it again. She'd looked happy until he had to go and spoil it by being sarcastic. He straightened and forced a smile as his mother stepped out of the barn and moseyed across the yard. She must be tired. Her usual stride was lively as a young'un's.

After his ma was seated and he'd climbed up beside her, she reached over and patted his hand. "What's wrong, dear? Why do you look so sad?"

Rafe sighed. Why did he even try to fool her? "Sorry, Ma. It's nothing."

She jiggled her fingers at Tuck and Addy as they drove past their wagon. "Rayford. Abby is a sweet girl, and I know you care for her. But she seems to have made her choice. I can't bear to see you suffering so. Especially when there are half a dozen girls standing in line for your attention."

He sighed. "Ma, I'm fine. You don't need to worry about me."

"I know and I won't, but I was just thinking about Carrie Sue Anderson. She's a very nice girl and pretty, too." She gave him a teasing smile and tapped him on the leg with her reticule. "And I know she's sweet on you."

"Ma, no matchmaking. Please." He knew he might as well be talking to the side of a barn. Ma thought he felt rejected and so she had to fix it for him.

She was dead right about his feeling rejected. He couldn't deny that. But he was pretty sure no one could fix it for him. Not even pretty, blond Carrie Sue with her enormous blue eyes and a dimple beside her mouth that just begged to be kissed. Tuck had ruined him for every other woman; no one else was like her. Whoever else he'd marry would always play second fiddle to Tuck.

He shook his head and flicked the reins to speed up the horses. He wouldn't coat his hurt ego by wooing another girl. Wouldn't be fair to her. . .whoever she might be. No, his original plan was better. He'd head down to Arkansas and join the railroad crew that was laying ties for the White River Line. By the time he worked his way back to these parts, Tuck would have married Sam Fields and it would be over and done with.

Pain knifed his heart. He stopped at the front step and helped Ma out of the wagon, then headed for the barn to do evening chores before supper.

❧

Tuck had always made fun of girls who swooned over a man. She'd scoffed and accused them of pretending. Now she wasn't so sure.

The feathery touch of Sam's lips brushing across her hand sent shivers through her body. She was pretty sure she was close to swooning herself.

"You're looking lovely today, my dear." Sam smiled, making no move to release her hand.

"Th–thank. . ." She cleared her throat. "Thank you."

He'd driven over to the farm in his new carriage, and now that supper was over, the two of them stood on the front porch watching the sunset.

"I thought perhaps you'd like to go for a drive." He squeezed her hand.

With a little tug, she gently removed it from his. After all, they weren't engaged yet. "I don't know. It will be dark soon." And Ma wouldn't approve at all.

"Just a short drive, then. We have plenty of time before it's actually dark." He gazed down at her, his eyes almost piercing her.

Fire shot through her body. How could he have such an effect on her? She shuddered. And how could he be so charming one moment and so disturbing the next? "I don't know, Sam."

A shadow crossed his face. "I've barely seen you at all lately, with my trips and medical practice. I would think you'd want to spend time with me."

Tuck bit her lip. She wasn't easily intimidated but felt almost powerless against his aggressive personality. She wanted to break free, and then again, she didn't. A part of her wanted to follow him wherever he wished to lead her.

"All right. Let me tell Ma and Pa we're leaving."

"Nonsense. We'll be back in a flash. They'll never even know we were gone."

Tuck sighed and surrendered. "All right. If you promise to bring me home in just a few minutes."

His face smoothed, and once more he flashed a bright smile. "Of course." He placed his hand beneath her elbow and helped her down the steps, as though she hadn't been running up and down them since she was a little girl.

She was pretty sure she could manage them without help. She was just about to step up into the carriage, when the front door opened and Pa stalked out onto the porch.

"What's going on here?" He glanced at Tuck then turned thunderous eyes on Sam.

Sam gave a nervous laugh. "We were only going for a short drive in my new carriage. I thought she would enjoy it."

Pa studied Sam for a moment. "I think you'd better wait for another time. It will be dark shortly."

Oh dear, this hadn't been a good idea at all. Pa looked like he was ready to knock Sam off the porch. She'd better do something. "Thank you so much, Sam, for coming to supper. I'd better get inside now. See you at church Sunday?" She made her voice as cheerful as she could and smiled brightly.

Sam nodded and bowed, then climbed into the carriage. Another shadow eclipsed his face, making her shudder.

With a troubled countenance, Papa Jack watched him drive away then turned and smiled at Tuck. "Let's go inside.

Your ma wanted to ask your opinion about something."

She found Ma and Addy bent over the kitchen table peering at some fabric samples.

"Oh, there you are, Tuck." Ma looked up. "Come help us decide on dress colors for the Christmas ball. Would you like this evergreen shade? Or perhaps this cranberry color?"

Tuck laughed. Ma always had such a delightful way of describing things. Never just red or green. "Isn't it a little early to decide? It's only October. We haven't had the harvest festival yet."

"But Christmastime will be here before we know it." Ma smiled, her eyes sparkling. Tuck wasn't sure if it was because of the baby or because Christmas was so near. Probably both.

Ma loved everything about Christmas. So did Rafe. Every year Ma and Mrs. Collins filled baskets for some of the neighbors, especially the older folks, and Tuck and Rafe delivered them. Her heart fluttered at the thought. Then she sighed. Another tradition she'd have to give up if she married Sam.

Perhaps Sam liked Christmas, too. If not, if he brooded, or worse still, made fun of their traditions, it would ruin it for her. But why wouldn't he like Christmas? She was being silly again. She didn't know why she allowed so many negative thoughts about Sam to enter her head lately.

eleven

"But Sam, you just got back from a week in St. Louis and now you're leaving again? You'll miss the festival." Tears threatened to spill over, and Tuck blinked hard, anger rising within her. She never cried. Well, hardly ever. She'd cried on Rafe's shoulder a few times, but that was different. And she cried sometimes when she got mad. Like now.

She'd ridden into town to pick up some sugar for Ma, and Sam had asked her to come to his office. Happy for his attention, she'd complied, only to be greeted with the news he had to go to Kansas City for two weeks.

"I know, sweetheart." He sounded as dejected as she felt, and her heart quickened at his use of the endearment. "But it can't be helped. My mother isn't as strong as she used to be and needs help with some business matters. I can't ignore her needs, now can I?"

Oh, he'd never mentioned his mother. Guilt bit at her. Hadn't she only recently promised God she wouldn't be so selfish? Here Sam was, trying to be a dutiful son, and she could only think about going to the festival without him. "Oh, of course not. Please forgive me. Certainly you must go to your mother's assistance."

Relief washed over his face. He took a step toward her, then darted a glance at the open door and stepped back. "I knew you would understand, my dear."

Amusement cut through Tuck's disappointment. Sam knew Mr. Hawkins would be watching and listening as long as Tuck was in the office.

"When will you leave?" Ma had given permission to invite

him for supper. At the time, Tuck hadn't even been sure she wanted to invite him, but now, disappointment washed over her. What was wrong with her anyway? She was turning into a double-minded simpleton where Sam was concerned.

"This afternoon, I'm afraid. I need to visit a family on the Forsyth road this morning. But I'll have to leave right afterwards." He smiled. "I can't wait to tell Mother about you. And when I return we'll do something special. I promise."

Her heart fluttered. She loved it when he was sweet like this. It didn't happen often enough to suit her. Quickly she pushed the thought away. After all, he was busy and had the care of most of the county on his shoulders. Perhaps she expected too much of him.

She returned Sam's smile. "That sounds wonderful. And don't worry about the festival. I'll go with my family and spend time with Addy and Rafe."

His eyes flashed with irritation. "I don't know why you have to hang around Rafe. How do you think that makes me feel? After all, you and I practically have an understanding."

That was news to her, but good news nevertheless. Satisfaction rippled through her. He really did care for her. She hadn't been sure before.

"Oh, Sam." She laughed. "Rafe and I have been best friends since we were children. There's never been anything more than that between us."

"Then I'm very sorry I allowed my jealousy to show. I know I can trust you. Now, my dear, I do need to make my rounds, so you need to run along." He took her hand and squeezed. "The two weeks will pass quickly. You'll see."

Being summarily dismissed, Tuck left his office and did her shopping, then stood outside the store and glanced around. This was practice day, and Tuck had missed her last two sessions with the oldsters. She always dropped whatever she was doing when Sam wanted her to do something with him. The troubling thought hit her unexpectedly. But he had so little free time and naturally they wanted to spend it together. She frowned. Still, he never seemed to mind that she would give up something important to her every time he showed up.

She retrieved her fiddle from beneath the wagon seat and headed over to the feed store. Mr. Willie and the rest were tuning up.

"Hey. Would you look here at what the cat drug in." Squeezebox slapped his leg and grinned good-naturedly in Tuck's direction.

" 'Bout time, too." Tom tried to look stern, but his sudden coughing spasm ruined the effect.

"I guess I could turn around and leave if you all don't want me here." Oh, there she went again. Snapping at them when she knew very well they were just teasing.

"Naw, don't leave," Mr. Willie soothed. He was always afraid someone would hurt her feelings. "They're jest foolin', Tuck."

Tuck looked up at the sky for a moment. "Well, all right. I reckon I'll stay then."

Squeezebox cackled. "All righty then, get her tuned up, girl. We ain't got all day."

Tom snorted. "Why not? You don't do anything else but lay around your shack snoring all day. You and that hound of yours."

"Hank don't snore." At the sound of his name, a flop-eared hound dog raised his head about an inch from the floor and then plopped it back down. Squeezebox scratched him behind one ear and then picked up his accordion.

Tuck removed her violin from the case and tuned up. "Okay, did we decide which one we're doing first?"

"I thought we'd start with 'Frog Went A-Courtin'" and

then 'Old Joe Clark.' Get everyone good and stirred up for the fun," Mr. Willie said. "That way, they'll likely buy more stuff and the ladies will have more money for the Christmas dance."

"Good thinking, Mr. Willie." Tuck grinned as she placed a soft cloth on her shoulder and her violin beneath her chin.

They ran through the two songs then went into a few more numbers they planned to play at the festival. Right in the middle of a soft rendition of "Sweet Adeline," a thunderous snore roared from Hank's direction, followed by the dog jumping up and howling loud and long.

The roar of laughter that followed nearly drowned out the dog.

⁂

Rafe swung the ax down hard, splitting the short logs for Ma's cookstove. Some of the neighbors were using oil stoves to cook on, but Ma said absolutely not. They'd have to be a sight better than they were now before she'd give up her woodstove. Rafe chuckled. Fine with him. The smell of bacon and eggs frying on that old stove was about the most tantalizing thing he'd ever had a sniff of. Except maybe Ma's fried chicken.

Horse's hooves sounded on the lane leading to the house. Rafe looked up. Tuck was almost lying down on Sweet Pea's neck as she urged her forward. That girl was going to break her neck one of these days if she didn't stop riding so hard. She'd gone flying a few times before, luckily escaping with scrapes and bruises.

"You trying to kill yourself or something?" He frowned as Tuck jumped down and sauntered toward him, a big grin on her face.

"You should talk. Who's the one who broke his collarbone twice and his arm three times, and what caused it?"

"Hey, one of those broken arms was from falling out of a

tree. You know that." But he grinned.

"Of course, I remember." She cocked her head and grinned. "But you were practicing jumping into the saddle from the branch of the old oak in the middle of our pasture. So it still involved a reckless act with a horse."

She had a point. "Okay, we're both lucky to be alive with all the shenanigans we pulled."

Laughing, she punched him on the arm. "Yep. You can say that again."

"Where's your fancy dress and hair geegaws?"

She shrugged. "No sense in torturing myself when Sam's not around to see me, is there?"

"Oh, the fancy doctor's gone again?"

"What's that supposed to mean?" She planted her hands on her hips and glared. "He has a perfectly good reason for being gone. Just like he always does."

Rafe snorted. "Listen to yourself, Tuck. Like he *always* does?"

"If you're going to make insinuations about Sam, I'm leaving." She spun around and stomped back to her horse.

Rafe exhaled loudly. Lately, all he seemed to do when they were together was to rile her up. "Come on, Tuck. Don't leave. I'm sorry, okay?"

She jumped on her horse. "Sure you are. I can see it all over you. I guess you forgot I told you I'm going to marry him. If you dislike him that much, I guess we can't be friends." She wheeled Sweet Pea around then yelled back over her shoulder, "And for your information, he's in Kansas City helping out his mother."

Rafe loaded up his arms with logs and stalked toward the house. Fine. If she could sling their friendship away that easily, so could he. There was no way he could pretend to like Sam Fields. He dumped the logs in the wooden box by the stove.

His mother looked up from the pan of potatoes she was slicing. "I thought I heard Abby. Didn't you invite her in?"

"She had to leave, Ma. I'm going over to the cave. I'll finish up the chores when I get back." He gave her a peck on the cheek.

As Champ's hooves thundered down the road, Rafe attempted to get his thoughts under control. He reckoned, somewhere in the back of his mind, he'd always figured he'd marry Tuck. There was no one else he'd rather be around. No one else who could make him laugh those roaring side-splitting howls of joy. No one who could calm him down with a word and melt his heart.

But that was then. Tuck had made her choice, and there was no use making himself miserable by thinking about it.

Anger roiled inside him. Who needed her? There were dozens of girls he could have. Carrie Sue's sweet smile crossed his thoughts. She had curls as yellow as a sunflower and eyes as blue as a spring sky. Also a sweet disposition. She wouldn't drive a man crazy with her wild and willful ways the way Tuck did. No sir. Carrie Sue would be there for her man and treat him the way a man wanted to be treated by his woman.

He turned his horse and headed for the Anderson farm. It was time for him to stop mooning over Tuck and get on with his life, and he intended to start right now. He hoped Carrie Sue didn't have an escort to the festival, because he'd like nothing better than to stroll past Tuck with Carrie on his arm.

Just before he reached the farm, he reined his horse in. What kind of idiot was he anyway? Planning on taking Carrie to the festival to get even with Tuck? That was the sort of thing a kid would do. He sighed. And Tuck probably wouldn't give a hoot anyway. With a heavy heart, he turned back toward home

Tuck laid her fiddle on a chair and stepped off the platform. Her stomach rumbled as she headed for the barn where tables were laden with food. The auction was winding up. She glanced at Rafe as he held up fingers to indicate a bid. Curious she peered at the auction stage to see what he was bidding on. A saddle. Looked like a good one, too. She looked back at him and he grinned.

They'd made their peace the day after their squabble. Both of them apologized. Rafe hadn't made any more comments about Sam. Tuck, on the other hand, was being careful not to mention him when she was with Rafe. Not an ideal compromise, but better than losing their friendship.

"Sold! To Carter Foster." The auctioneer's voice boomed across the barn, and Rafe shrugged and went to help move the benches and make room for tables.

Tuck waited until he was finished and grabbed his hand. "C'mon, I'm starving." She dragged him across to a table holding platters of fried chicken and bowls filled with potato salad and corn on the cob. With plates piled high, they found two empty spots at a table.

"Hello, Rafe. You must be hungry, judging by that plate of yours."

At the sound of the lilting voice, Tuck peered around Rafe and saw Carrie Sue Anderson sitting on the other side of him.

"I sure am." Rafe smiled at the pretty blond. "I'm hungry enough to eat a horse."

Her rippling laughter grated on Tuck's nerves. "Oh no, you won't need to do that. My mama and I brought plenty of fried chicken. And we're mighty good cooks, if I do say so myself." Tuck glared at her, and she tossed her head and added, "I notice you have rather a hearty appetite as well, Abigail."

"The name is Tuck. And what's wrong with an appetite?"

"Why, nothing at all, if you want to blow up and look like the side of a barn." She smiled sweetly, and Tuck felt sick. "A lady must be careful you know."

"A good thing I don't care about being a lady then," Tuck retorted.

The gasp from behind her had to be Addy. No one else could gasp like that. "Abby, of course you don't mean that. You're very much a lady. Just a high-spirited one." She glanced around for a place at their table.

Rafe stood. "Here, take my place, Addy. Jim just came in and I need to talk to him about something."

Tuck stared as he bolted across to the door where Jim had stopped to talk to some of the men. Now why did he take off so fast? She turned and saw Carrie gazing after him, with the expression of a sick cow.

Oh. So that's what was going on. Carrie was after Rafe, and he was well aware of it.

twelve

"Here, let me wrap this blanket around you, my dear." Tuck blushed as Sam spread the thick gray blanket across her legs and tucked it a little too closely for her comfort.

"Sam, the blanket is fine. Please. Leave it alone." Tuck scooted away and tugged the blanket loose. Didn't he understand propriety at all?

"Sorry, I simply don't want you to be cold. I didn't mean to embarrass you." Sam's eyes darkened, a warning he was irritated. Well, so was she.

"Where are we going? It's too cold for a buggy ride, anyway. We should have stayed home and played games with Ma and Pa and Addy." Tuck's heart thumped hard and fast. What was wrong with her? This was Sam and he loved her. Of course he didn't mean to be inappropriate.

"Must you spend all your time with your family, Abigail?" he snapped. "Can't we ever have time to ourselves? Even for a simple ride in the countryside?"

She stared at him. Was she being unreasonable or was he? She enjoyed doing things with her family. But if she was going to be Sam's wife, she would need to put his wishes first. And he had made it plain he didn't like being around them a lot. What if he refused to let her spend time with them after they were married? Of course, he hadn't actually asked her to marry him, but she was certain he would soon. Maybe that's why he wanted to be alone now.

She brightened and sat up straight, placing a hand on his forearm. "I'm sorry. I'm being selfish. Of course I want to spend time with you."

"Well, that's more like it." He placed his hand over hers and smiled. His glance intensified as he looked deep into her eyes, but the expression that used to send thrills through her only made her uneasy.

Sam flicked the reins and drove to the river, following the old horse path that rumor said was an old Indian trail.

"Where will the White River Line tracks be, Sam? Will we still have access to the river?" Tuck shivered. She couldn't imagine not going fishing with Rafe. Confusion washed over her. She wouldn't be allowed to fish or float on the river with Rafe much longer. Or do anything with him for that matter. Not when she was Sam's wife.

"I know absolutely nothing about the railroad except it's a lot more comfortable riding in trains than on horseback or in coaches clear across the country." He softened his tone and smiled. "You would love the train. They even have dining cars where they serve the finest cuisine."

She laughed as she tried to visualize eating on the train. "How good can food be cooked in a moving car? I'll bet it's not nearly as good as Ma's chicken. And Sam, have you ever eaten trout cooked over an open fire? There's absolutely nothing like it."

His face wrinkled with distaste. "No, I haven't and have no intention of trying it. Really, Abigail. Have you no desire at all for the finer things of life?"

She sighed. For the first time she admitted to herself that she and Sam had little in common. But they loved each other. That was all that mattered. "It's getting dark. We really need to get back to the house before Ma and Pa start to worry."

"All right. All right. Soon. I promise. Let's just stop and look at the river for a moment." His voice sounded distracted and strange as he pulled off the path.

"But Sam, it's cold, and my hands are like ice." She

shivered, not sure if it was entirely from the cold.

But Sam had already stopped the horses and set the carriage brake. He turned and smiled. "Here, let me see those hands."

"No, they're all right. Let's just look at the river for a moment. Did you have something you wanted to talk about?" She waited, expecting him to bring up the subject of their future.

He reached over and brushed a curl from her forehead. "You're so beautiful, Abigail. I didn't realize it the first time I saw you, with you in those awful overalls. What a pleasant surprise it was when you appeared in my office that day, transformed into a stunning lady."

"I'm happy you are pleased with my appearance. But I'm the same person as I was in the overalls." For some reason, it was important for her to make that clear. She'd been pretending with him for too long.

"Nonsense. Not at all, my dear. Now you're a woman. A very alluring woman." He moved over closer to her on the seat and placed an arm around her shoulders, pulling her close.

"Sam, what are you doing?" She pulled back, but the side of the carriage stopped her retreat.

"Don't be shy, my dear. After all, we've been seeing each other for some time. A kiss would be quite appropriate. Don't you think?"

His lips were almost touching hers now. Without another thought, she gave him a shove backward then slapped him hard.

"Why, you little—" Venomous rage filled his voice and his eyes blazed with anger. He made a move as if to lift his arm.

Tuck gasped. He was going to hit her. She balled up her hand into a fist, and a rush of anger exploded within her. Let him just dare.

He drew his hand back and swiped it across his face as though wiping away the sting of her slap. His breath came in angry spurts, and his eyes knifed through her, furious and threatening. Grabbing the reins, he tore off down the road, not slowing until he jerked the team to a halt at her front porch. As soon as Tuck had jumped out of the carriage, he laid the whip across the backs of his horses.

Tuck, with her heart racing, ran up the steps and into the house. She leaned against the door, letting her pulse and breathing calm down. It wouldn't do to let anyone see her like that.

The house was silent, but a dim light shone from the parlor.

Forcing a smile upon her stiff face, she paused at the parlor door long enough to say good night to Ma and Pa. She scurried away and up the stairs before they could speak.

Could she fool Addy? They'd always shared a room, enjoying the late night talks, but at this moment, Tuck wished one of them had taken over the guest room.

As Tuck walked into the bedroom, Addy, lying in bed, glanced up and smiled, laying aside the magazine she was reading. "How was your ride? I was beginning to worry a little."

"Oh, it was fine. There was no reason for you to be concerned. It's only just now getting dark." She hung her cloak on a hook and sat in the rocking chair by the window. The memory of the rage on Sam's face when she slapped him sent her heart racing again. If he'd made a move, she'd have socked him a good one.

"Abby, what's wrong?" Her sister threw her legs over the side of the bed and slipped her feet into a pair of crocheted slippers.

"Nothing is wrong. What makes you think something is wrong?" Her voice sounded frantic even to her own ears, and her heartbeat pounded in her ears.

"Oh, maybe because you're rocking so furiously. If you go much faster, that chair is going to fly out the window."

Chagrined, Tuck stopped rocking. Okay, she could do this. She took a long, slow breath and then threw a grin at her sister. "The window is closed. I do believe the rocking chair is quite safe."

Addy pressed her lips together. "You can't fool me. I know something happened to upset you."

"Well, you're wrong." She yawned and stood so fast she set the chair to rocking back and forth again. "I'm sleepy. That's all. Don't worry about me so much." Without another word, she changed into her nightgown and crawled beneath the pile of quilts. "Good night, Addy."

She lay still, and slowly, moment by moment, her anger dissipated. What if Sam's attempt to kiss her wasn't as awful as she had built it up to be? After all, he mentioned an understanding, so obviously he intended to marry her. Then why did she have this sinking feeling inside her?

Until he actually declared his intentions, a kiss was out of the question and inappropriate as well as disrespectful to her. If Sam treated her with disrespect now, how could she expect him to treat her if they should marry? She wished she could talk this over with someone. Ordinarily, Addy was her confidant, but telling her about this was out of the question.

Rafe's face, safe and friendly, popped into her mind. Immediately she pushed the thought away. Rafe would likely tell her she was a fool to even consider forgiving Sam. And then he'd go beat the tar out of him.

❧

Rafe shivered as the wind whipped around the house and nearly knocked him over. He grabbed Addy and steadied her. He'd invited her inside, but she'd insisted she needed to talk to him in private. His mother might think it strange that

Addy was here to see Rafe without her sister.

"Let's at least go stand by the barn where we'll be shielded. You're not even wearing a coat." He frowned as he glanced at the shawl wrapped loosely around Addy's shoulders. If it was Tuck, he'd just go inside the barn, but Addy would think it was inappropriate.

"It wasn't this cold when I left the house. How was I supposed to know a norther was going to hit?" She followed him across the yard to the shielded side of the big, weathered structure.

"Before you leave, I'm going to find a cloak or something for you to wear on the way home." He didn't need anything else on his conscience, like Tuck's sister catching pneumonia.

"There's a blanket in the wagon. I can use that." Addy stomped her small foot, and wrinkles puckered the skin between her eyes. "Stop fussing, Rafe. I need to talk to you."

"I'm sorry." Rafe frowned. He should've noticed how nervous Addy seemed. Maybe someone was ill. Dread washed over him. "Is Tuck all right?"

She took a deep breath. "I'm not sure. She says she's fine, but she's been behaving strangely ever since she went for a carriage ride with Sam a few days ago."

Rafe's stomach twisted and knotted, and he tightened his lips. "Have you questioned her?"

"Of course I've questioned her. She just laughs or gets angry and tells me to stop fussing over her. She insists everything is fine." Addy twisted the handkerchief in her hand. "Rafe, I don't trust that man."

Worry niggled its way inside Rafe's mind. Addy knew Tuck better than anyone, except maybe him. If she thought something was wrong, she was likely right. Of course, this was the first time Tuck had taken up with some man. That might change things. There could be some things she just didn't want to share with her sister, and maybe some of those things weren't so good. He licked his dry lips.

He'd always thought Tuck pretty levelheaded, but she'd fallen pretty hard for Fields. His chest tightened. He didn't trust him either. He never had since he'd first laid eyes on him. He wasn't sure why, couldn't quite put his finger on anything really wrong. He'd finally decided it was jealousy on his part. But now, with Addy saying the same thing, he wasn't so certain. Surely the man hadn't taken liberties with her. Naw, she'd have come straight to Rafe and told him. Wouldn't she?

"Look, Addy. I don't know what I can do. Tuck's not talking to me the way she used to. Why don't you talk to your pa?" Yes, that would be the sensible thing. Jack would check it out.

"Because, I don't know what Pa would do. Probably go straight to Abby and confront her. Then she'd never speak to me again." She bit her lip and blinked back tears. It was obvious this wasn't just a small concern to her.

"All right. Let me think about this. I'm not sure what I can do, but I'll figure out something. If anything is wrong, I promise I'll find out. Trust me?" He laid his hand on her shoulder, and it felt so much like Tuck's he jerked his hand away.

Addy smiled. "Of course I trust you. Why would I have come here otherwise? I know how much you care about Abby. I wish she would open her eyes, because I know she cares about you, too, Rafe."

He smiled. "I know she does. Like a brother or something."

"I think you're wrong, Rafe. You mean a great deal more than that to her. She just doesn't realize it yet." She placed her hand, so much like Tuck's, on his arm. "Don't give up on her."

He sighed. "I don't know, Addy. Sometimes it seems hopeless, and I think I'm an idiot to keep hoping she could ever love me."

"Well, if anyone is an idiot, it's Abby, not you. I hope she finds out before it's too late."

"Me, too. But the important thing now is to figure out what's going on. Don't worry. If anything is wrong, I'll take care of it."

As he watched her drive away, Rafe sent up a silent prayer that he could keep his promise.

thirteen

The store was dark in spite of the oil lamps placed around the big room. Tuck hated these cloudy days when she didn't know if it was going to pour down rain or not. Especially when she and the oldsters had a practice. She walked to the post office at the rear of the store. She needed to mail Pa's letter before she did Ma's shopping. Otherwise she'd probably forget.

There was no sign of the manager in the store or behind the post office window. He must be in the storage room. She laid the letter on the counter in front of the window where he would find it. She'd pay for the stamp after she finished shopping.

As she walked over to the dry goods section, the front door opened and Sam walked in. She caught her breath. She hadn't seen him since the attempted kiss and what followed.

He saw her and started toward her.

She stiffened, not knowing what to expect or even what she wanted him to do or say as he stopped in front of her.

"I'm so sorry, Abigail. I don't know what came over me. Maybe it was the moonlight shining on your hair. I guess I lost control for a moment." Sam gave her a contrite and pleading glance. Like she'd fall for that.

She stared, not sure what to say. She didn't want to assume he was lying, but she couldn't forget his cold rage and her suspicion he wanted to hit her.

"Say something, please. Tell me you forgive me." He smiled sadly. And the expression on his face seemed sincere.

"What about the fit you threw?"

He looked away then back. "I was shocked when you slapped me, although you had every right to do so. I think that, combined with the realization of what I'd done, caused me to lose control."

"For a moment, I thought you would hit me." Again, anger began to boil inside her. He would have been in for a surprise if he had. She took a deep breath. Who was she kidding? He was a lot stronger than she was.

"Oh no, Abby, please don't think I would ever harm a hair of your head, my dear. You're much too precious to me." She avoided the hand he reached out for hers. "And of course, I wouldn't strike any woman on any account."

She swallowed. Should she believe him? Trust him? As he looked at her with those deep, searching eyes, her resolve began to melt. Perhaps she should give him a second chance. He deserved that, didn't he? After all, everyone needed a second chance now and then. "All right, Sam. I forgive you. But if anything similar should ever happen again, don't come near me or even attempt to speak to me."

This time when he reached for her hand, she made no move to avoid it.

The smile on his face seemed real enough. Although there was a possibility he was manipulating her, she needed to give him a chance. The Bible did say something about forgiving others when they asked you to.

"Let's celebrate. Come on back to the office. Mrs. Carey brought me a delicious apple cobbler yesterday, and it hasn't been touched yet." He flashed her a grin. "We'll leave the door open of course."

"I'm sorry, I need to do my mother's shopping and go practice with the group." A thrill of victory ran through her for not changing her plans. There. Let him chew on that.

Disappointment washed over his face. "Very well. Another time then. May I drive you to church on Sunday?"

"Yes, I suppose that would be all right." She nodded then turned to the dry goods on the shelf.

"Good day, then." She listened as his footsteps crossed the floor and the door opened and closed.

Anxious to get to the feed store before the group started practicing without her, she hurried through her shopping then paid Mr. Hawkins for the stamp. A little twinge of excitement ran through her as she thought of the Christmas ball which was only a few weeks away. They'd be playing again for this one, but she meant to stop in plenty of time to have some fun herself. After all, the oldsters had been playing music for a long time before she came into the group, and she had a right to have some fun, too.

As she walked out the door, Rafe rode up. He grinned and waved as he dismounted.

"Tuck, what are you up to?"

The sound of his voice rippled through her entire body. She felt laughter well up inside.

"Rafe! Getting ready to go practice with the gang. It's good to see you. Why haven't you been by?"

"Well, I figure you're busy now that the doc is courting you." He grinned, but it didn't quite reach his eyes.

"I'm never too busy for old friends. I thought maybe Carrie Sue had you all roped and tied."

He chuckled. "Nope. Don't know why you'd think that."

"Huh! The way she was hanging all over you at the festival could be one reason." She peered at him closely to see his reaction. Maybe he liked having Carrie crazy over him. "It's obvious she's after you."

His eyes glinted, and he laughed again. "Tell you what. If she ever catches me, you'll be the first to know." He gave her a wave and went inside.

She loaded her things into the wagon and covered them with a tarp in case it rained. Then she headed down to the feed store. Her thoughts turned to Sam, but they were different than they were a few weeks ago. Oh, he was still handsome and he could be charming, but she no longer felt weak-kneed when she saw him.

When had her feelings begun to change? It was before the incident by the river. She sighed. Of course feelings would change when the new wore off a relationship. She still loved Sam. It just felt different.

She'd always thought love would be a happy feeling, but being with Rafe just now was the happiest she'd been in a long time. Why couldn't Sam make her feel like that?

a

"Hello there, Rafe. Forget something when you were in here yesterday?" Mr. Hawkins came out from behind the post office cubicle and held out his hand.

Rafe shook his hand, silently gloating over Tuck's first sign of jealousy. If he wasn't imagining it. "No, sir. Don't need a thing. Is the doc in?"

"You're in luck. He just came in from a house call a few minutes ago, and as far as I know he doesn't have a patient in there with him." Mr. Hawkins motioned toward the doctor's office. "You ailing with something?"

"Just a sore neck and shoulder." He felt a slight pang at the lie. Actually, he'd had a sore neck the week before, but it was fine now except for a twinge now and then. It gave him a good excuse to go see Fields though. He went back to the doctor's office and knocked, then opened the door.

Fields appeared cautious when he saw Rafe step through the door.

Suspicion wrapped itself around Rafe's mind. Why would the doc be concerned about him? Except that he knew Rafe was Tuck's friend as well as a friend of the family.

"What can I do for you, Collins?" Fields stepped forward, a questioning look on his face.

"My neck and shoulder have been giving me fits. May have strained something hauling wood to Forsyth." That much was true. He didn't have to tell the man it was pretty much healed up. "Thought maybe I should have you check it out."

The doctor motioned to a wooden stool. "Why don't you sit over there and take your shirt off? I'll take a look."

Rafe obliged and sat while the doctor probed his shoulder and examined his neck. He refused to flinch, even when Fields's fingers dug into a tender spot.

"Hmmm. I can't find anything out of place. You're probably right about the strain." He stood back and looked at Rafe. His mouth twisted and his eyes bore into Rafe's.

Was that a knowing look on his face? Probably just Rafe's imagination. Why would Fields suspect anything? Rafe was another patient, and a paying one at that. That was all.

While Rafe put his shirt on, the doctor walked over to a cabinet and took out a bottle of liniment. "Here, rub this on the sore spots a couple of times a day. It'll help a little. Mainly you just have to wait it out though. It'll get better."

Rafe nodded. "Thanks, what do I owe you?"

He handed the amount Sam mentioned over to the doctor, then took the bottle and headed out the door. What a waste. He hadn't learned a thing. Although he had no idea what he'd expected to find out from a doctor's visit.

He went outside and glanced at the liniment in his hand. This was silly. They had jugs of the stuff at home. He might as well leave it here for someone else. He turned and walked back into the office.

Fields, his back to the door, stood by his phone and laughed softly into the mouthpiece. "I love you, my dear. You do know that, don't you?"

Rafe inhaled sharply then held his breath. Now who was the doctor professing his love to? Maybe this visit wouldn't be such a waste after all.

Fields spoke into the phone again. "Yes, of course. I'll see you soon. Very soon. Yes. Good-bye, my sweet."

Rafe turned and slipped out the door before the doctor turned around.

Was the conversation what it sounded like? If so, he felt like giving the guy a good trouncing for the hurt Tuck was going to feel when she found out.

He waved at Hawkins and left the store again, a thunder roaring in his brain. How did he think she was going to find out? He sure couldn't tell her. She'd probably think he was making it up, although there was no reason why she'd think that when she didn't know how he felt about her.

Champ whinnied when he stepped over to untie him. He patted the horse and slipped him a lump of sugar before mounting.

Bothered by the conversation, he rode toward home. How could he handle this? The doctor could be totally innocent. Rafe'd only heard a couple of sentences. Maybe it was the man's mother he was talking to. But his voice when he said I love you wasn't the tone a man used when he spoke to his ma or his sister. It had been downright seductive. No, he was talking to a sweetheart.

Which brought Rafe back to his problem. How could he handle this in a way where Tuck wouldn't get hurt? Even if his suspicions were true, it wasn't his place to reveal it to her. He should probably talk to Addy. But he hated to give her more to worry about.

He turned toward the Sullivan farm, urging Champ forward. He needed to speak to Jack about this. Tuck's pa would know how to handle it. He didn't know how long Tuck would be in town. From the look of the sky, probably not too long. He needed to hurry and talk to Jack and leave before she got home.

Reining his horse in, he jumped off and tied him to the

front porch rail. He knocked on the door and after a minute heard footsteps.

Lexie opened the door and smiled. "Come in, Rafe. How nice to see you."

Lexie was the happiest person he knew. And she always acted as if she hadn't seen him in weeks, even if it had been the day before.

"Thanks, it sure smells good in here." Grinning, he sniffed in appreciation of the sweet, fruity aroma.

The corners of her eyes crinkled with pleasure. "That's my apple cobbler you smell. And it'll be cool enough to dish up in a few minutes."

Rafe shook his head. "Wish I could, but I need to talk to Jack then hurry home. It looks like it might storm, and I'll have to help Pa get the animals into the barn."

"You'll find him in the barn. I have no idea what he's doing, but I'm sure he'll be happy to see you." She patted him on the arm. "I'll save you some cobbler to take home for you and your folks. There's plenty."

"Thank you, ma'am. I'm obliged. I'll just go out there now." With one more breath of longing for the cobbler, he crossed the yard to the barn.

The sound of "Amazing Grace" greeted him as he walked into the barn. Jack sat on a bale of hay, singing at the top of his lungs, while he polished an old saddle.

"Hey, Jack."

Jack Sullivan glanced up and grinned when he saw Rafe. "Come on in, boy. I'm glad for some male company. All those women talk about is dresses and geegaws for the Christmas dance. I had to escape to the barn for my sanity."

Rafe laughed. "Yes, I can imagine. I think all the ladies in the county have gone a little bit Christmas crazy. And it's still only the middle of November."

"What brings you out on a day like this? It's likely going to storm within the hour." He frowned. "I hope Tuck makes it back before it hits."

"I saw her in town about an hour ago. She was going over to practice but didn't plan to stay long." Rafe looked at the ground then back at Jack. "I really need to talk to you about something. And it just might concern Tuck, sir."

fourteen

A lilting feeling tickled Tuck's stomach, and laughter bubbled up inside her as she noticed Champ tied up by the barn. Rafe was here. Apparently he'd come to see Papa Jack, but maybe he'd stay for supper and they could have a long talk afterward.

She stopped in front of the house to make it quicker and easier to unload the wagon. Jumping down, she headed across the yard. Rafe would help her carry things inside.

The barn door was open a crack, and Rafe's voice drifted out. "At first I sort of gave him the benefit of the doubt, thinking maybe he was talking to his mother or sister. But believe me, that tone of voice wasn't the way a man speaks to his ma. I wanted to drag him outside and teach him a lesson he wouldn't forget. The idea of him toying with Tuck like that while all the time he's got a sweetheart somewhere. . ."

Tuck's breath caught in her chest, and pain shot though her. Rafe could only be talking about Sam. But. . .what did he mean? Sam loved another woman? Surely it was a misunderstanding.

"Tell me again what Fields said. Maybe it wasn't as bad as you think." Pa's voice of reason fell like a healing balm on her ears.

She listened as Rafe, his voice tight with anger, repeated word for word what he said he'd heard.

"Now calm down, Rafe." Pa still spoke with quiet reason, but an underlying hint of suppressed anger revealed his real feelings. "I know you're angry, the way you care about Tuck. I am, too. But you need to be sure before you say anything to her."

"Say something to Tuck? You should know I can't be the one to tell her. Not with me being in love with her. It would just seem like jealousy on my part." Rafe's voice shook with emotion. "Anyway, she's changed so much, I hardly know her anymore."

Shock hit her. Fire centered in her forehead and spread outward and down her entire body. Shame and delight battled within her. How could she have fallen for Sam's lies when all the time he was courting someone else? But Rafe... Rafe loved her? Confusion swirled in her mind, twisting and intertwining with the other emotions.

She spun around and ran to the house. She couldn't let Rafe see her like this. He would know she'd overheard him. She stopped at the porch, her breath coming in gulps. She had to calm down before she went inside.

She began unloading the wagon and placing things on the porch. That would calm her down. Besides, it would seem odd if she left a wagon with supplies standing in front of the porch. Ma must not suspect anything was amiss. With a smile on her face, she carried some of the household supplies inside.

Ma and Addy were in the kitchen preparing the evening meal. "Abigail, I was beginning to worry that you'd be caught in a thunderstorm." Ma glanced at her and smiled.

Addy hurried over. "Here, let me take one of those baskets. Your arms are piled high."

"Just set them on the pantry floor, girls. We'll put them away after supper," Ma directed.

Just as Tuck was about to return to the wagon to get the remaining basket and the sack of flour, Pa came in the front door, carrying everything.

"Why didn't you call me to help, Tuck? I was right in the barn."

"Oh, I saw Rafe's horse and figured you two were talking. I didn't want to disturb you." A poor excuse, as her pa's puzzled expression confirmed. Ordinarily she'd have simply barged into the barn and dragged Rafe out to help.

"Abigail, get that covered bowl off the dough table and take it out to Rafe. I told him I'd send apple cobbler home with him."

Panic rose in Tuck. She groped around in her mind for an excuse.

Pa shook his head. "He's already gone. Wanted to beat the storm home. I guess he forgot about the cobbler."

Relief washed over Tuck. She'd have to see him sooner or later, but there was no way she could face Rafe now. How could she? Knowing he loved her and that he didn't know she knew. It was an impossible situation.

She frowned. Why did he have to go and ruin their friendship by falling in love with her? And why'd he have to spy on Sam? He'd probably got it all wrong anyway.

But something stirred deep inside her. A warmth unlike any she'd felt before.

After they'd eaten and the dishes were washed, Ma and Pa settled in the parlor. Ma with her sewing and Pa with a rifle that needed to be cleaned. Addy and Abby put the supplies away in the pantry.

"You're awfully quiet, Abby. Is something wrong?" Addy threw her a glance filled with curiosity.

Tuck leaned against the wall. She and Addy had always stuck together. As far as she knew, they'd never kept secrets from each other until recently, and that was Tuck's doing. She knew that Addy loved her, and although she loved her sister, too, Tuck also knew that her twin had been kinder to her through the years than she'd been in return.

Suddenly, she missed the talks they used to have, the laughter they'd shared. When had they lost it? Tuck sighed. She knew she was the one to blame. She'd pulled back from Addy out of jealousy. Addy had a sweet disposition that drew people to her. Tuck, on the other hand, knew she'd always been selfish. "I'd like to talk to you about something later."

"All right," Addy said, a question in her voice. "Let's finish up here and go to our room."

They finished putting the supplies away then went to the parlor to say good night to their parents.

Pa and Ma looked up when they came in. They both had worried expressions on their faces.

"Tuck, your mother and I would like to talk to you about something in private," Pa said.

Tuck took a deep breath. Here it was. It had to be about Rafe's accusation against Sam.

"All right, Pa." Tuck sat on the stool in front of her mother's rocking chair and waited while Addy said good night and went to their room.

Papa Jack cleared his throat. "Abigail, your mother and I know you are a young woman and old enough to make your own decisions, but we think your relationship with Dr. Fields is moving too fast."

Tuck licked her lips. How could she handle this? She couldn't let Pa know she'd overheard the part about Sam without also revealing she'd overheard Rafe's declaration of love. She swallowed. "What do you mean, Pa?"

Pa took a deep breath and looked at Ma. She placed her hand on his arm and nodded.

Tuck sat, frozen, and listened to the story once more. How should she respond? She hadn't yet had the time to think it over. She'd hoped her talk with Addy would help. She cleared her throat. "I'm not sure I believe it to be true."

"Abigail," Ma said, "surely you don't think Rafe would make up a story like that."

"No, of course not," Tuck said, frowning. "But he may have misunderstood. I think Sam at least deserves a chance to explain. Don't you?"

"Yes, certainly," Pa said quickly. "But how will you know if he's being honest?"

"I don't know, Pa. I guess I'll have to trust God to show me, won't I?"

The misery on her parents' faces stabbed her like a knife. Sharp and cruel. And suddenly she knew. They felt her pain.

"I promise I won't marry Sam Fields unless I can do so with your blessing and your assurance that all is well." They could count on that. Tuck wasn't sure if the pain she felt was grief or anger, but she knew she had to find out the truth about Sam.

ಸಲ

When Tuck walked into her bedroom, she found Addy seated in front of the stove in one of their twin rockers. She glanced up from the hem she was mending and smiled. "You still rip more hems than anyone I know, in spite of your new ladylike ways."

"You shouldn't be doing my mending for me, Addy. It's time I started doing things for myself."

"I needed something to do while I waited for you." She bit the thread and tied a knot, then handed the dress to Tuck with a smile.

Tuck tossed it on the bed and sat in the rocker beside her sister. She held her hands toward the stove, enjoying the warmth that enveloped them. "Sis, I don't know if I'll ever really be ladylike. I pretend really well when it suits me then go right back to my old ways."

"You're doing better," Addy said. "Don't put yourself down."

"But to tell the truth, I miss being me. Oh, I know I need to work on some things, but in doing so I'm not sure who I am anymore."

"You're our own precious Abigail Kentucky Sullivan, that's who. And I think you're just fine the way you are." She wrinkled her brow and bit her lip. "I know I nagged at you about changing, but I would never want you to stop being yourself."

"Well, obviously Sam doesn't feel that way." She leaned her head back

Addy frowned. "What do you mean? What did he say?"

"Nothing. Not to me, that is." Pain ripped through her, and she thought she'd be sick. "It seems Rafe overheard him talking to someone on the phone. A woman. He told her he loved her."

Addy's mouth dropped opened, and then she pressed her lips together. Her face crumpled.

Tuck frowned. "What? What were you going to say?"

"Nothing," Addy hastened to say. "Perhaps Rafe misunderstood. Tell me exactly what he said."

She repeated everything she'd overheard. "Do you think it's possible Rafe misunderstood?"

"Well, it's possible." Addy's face was washed with misery.

"But you don't think so."

"Well, no." She licked her lips.

Tuck stood and looked down at Addy, peering into her eyes. She knew her sister well enough to know she was hiding something. She'd suspected as much for some time but had shoved the suspicion aside. "Addy, you know something you aren't telling me."

Addy's face crumpled, and she placed her hands over her face. "I should have told you before."

Tuck reached down and pulled them away. Addy's eyes were full of tears.

"Just tell me, Addy. Tell me now."

"I've been so miserable." Addy jumped up and clutched Tuck's shoulders. "At first I thought it was my imagination telling me Sam was making advances toward me. A wink here, a suggestive smile there. But it didn't stop. Then one day when I was leaving the store, he approached me and asked me to go for a drive with him. I told him in no uncertain terms what I thought of him for that. And, Abby, he behaved the same way on different occasions to Phyllis Carter and Jane White."

Tuck stood frozen. A roaring in her ears drowned out the rest of what Addy was saying. *Please, God. Help me.* Suddenly clarity returned, and she heard her sister's voice loud and clear.

"Abby, are you all right? Should I get Ma?"

"No, no. Don't get Ma." She sat in her rocker. "But why didn't you tell me? Why would you keep such a thing from me?"

Addy dropped her hands and shook her head. "I'm so sorry. I don't know why I didn't tell you. Except, I didn't want to hurt you and I wasn't even sure you'd believe me."

Tuck closed her eyes for a moment. Would she have believed her? Sam had shown more interest in Addy than her at the beginning. She'd been jealous, and even after he started courting her, she still felt unkindly to Addy. Her jealousy must have shown through. No wonder her sister had been afraid to tell her about Sam's advances.

She stood and pulled Addy to her, wrapping her in her arms. "I'm so sorry. I should never have let anyone come between us. Can you forgive me?"

"Oh, Abby." Addy squeezed her tightly. "I've missed you so much."

They talked long into the night. And between tears and laughter, the bond that had always been between them grew stronger.

But there was one more question that Tuck knew she needed an answer for. "Addy, I know you had feelings for Sam in the beginning. And he was interested in you. I shouldn't have gone after him the way I did." She paused before continuing. "Do you still have those feelings?"

Addy drew back in horror. "Heavens, no! When I noticed how he treated you and how rude he could be, any feelings I had for him dissipated. I don't want to hurt you, Abby, but quite frankly, I can barely tolerate the man, and I know he's not good enough for you."

After Addy had fallen asleep, Tuck lay awake, her thoughts twisting inside her mind. What now? Although she never wanted to see Sam again, she knew she needed to confront him. He had a right to answer the accusations, although she doubted he could defend himself against them. Neither Rafe nor Addy would have lied about it. And she couldn't think of any plausible explanation that could make him innocent.

Finally, although she tried hard to keep it at bay, the memory of Rafe's declaration of love for her filled her thoughts. She had no idea how she felt about that or what to do about it, but it filled her heart with awe.

fifteen

After a restless night, Tuck got up early and slipped out to the barn to saddle Sweet Pea. The storm had ended, but light rain continued to fall. Ma would have been sure to protest Tuck's riding off to town.

A cold drizzle fell on Tuck and Sweet Pea as she rode fast and hard toward Branson's. She pulled up in front and, after taking care of Sweet Pea, went inside.

Only one customer browsed the aisles of the store. Tuck glanced around and saw Mr. Hawkins stocking the top shelves. Tuck walked quietly to Sam's office and tapped on the door.

Sam started when he saw her. Scorn twisted his face as his eyes took in her overalls. "Abby. What a surprise. Please come in."

Tuck kicked the door closed behind her and slipped past him, avoiding his hand that he held out toward her.

"Whatever will Mr. Hawkins say, my dear?" He flashed her a nervous smile. When she didn't return it, a thoughtful look crossed his face.

"I understand I'm not your only dear." The calmness of her voice surprised her. It certainly didn't match her desire to scratch his eyes out.

"Why would you say such a thing? Have you seen me with anyone else?" He frowned. The hurt expression on his face would have fooled her a few weeks ago.

"I have my reasons, Sam. I know you've made advances toward other women." She took a deep breath. "Did you really think you could get away with it, when I know most of the girls in the county?"

"Abigail, I don't know who has been telling these tales, but I assure you they are nothing but lies. I've hardly looked at another woman since I met you."

She shook her head. "You are pathetic. And how dare you call my sister a liar."

"Ah. Well, there you have it. She always was attracted to me." He chuckled. "Just a little case of jealousy."

She planted her hands on her hips and glared. "It's no use, Sam. Stop lying. Besides, someone heard you on the phone yesterday when you were professing your love to someone in quite a provocative voice."

A trapped look crossed his face. Then understanding dawned, and he laughed. A very unpleasant laugh. "Ah, I see. Caught by your devoted Rafe Collins. I don't suppose I could convince you he's making a mountain out of a molehill."

"No, you can't." *Thank You, God, for this peace.*

"Well then, I suppose I must confess. I like pretty women. Never could resist them." He smiled. "I actually was quite taken with your sister at first, I will admit."

"Then why did you turn your attentions to me?" The weasel. How could she have thought he had charm?

"Why, you were very entertaining, dear Abigail. It fascinated me that you were so enamored of me. You actually managed to turn yourself from a backwoods hillbilly into a lovely young lady. Of course, you still have rough spots, but perhaps someday those will smooth out."

"I see. So you were simply playing with my affections, leading me to believe that you were an honorable man who wanted to marry me." She stomped her foot. "Not that I'd marry a snake like you."

"Marry you?" Laughter exploded from his mouth. "Let me tell you a little secret, my dear. I couldn't marry you if I wished to, which I don't. You see, I'm already wed to the daughter of a very famous surgeon in Kansas City. In fact, we worked out some of our little problems when I was there recently, and I'm sure we'll be reuniting very soon."

She gasped. "You vile man. My pa will tar and feather you when he hears about this. And so will every other man in the neighborhood. You'll be run out of town faster than you can say, 'my dear' anything."

"Hmmm, you may have a point there. And I'm sure your Rafe will lead the pack. Well then, I was bored with this place at any rate, so perhaps I'd best say adieu. There are plenty of other communities in need of a doctor."

Tuck gave a short laugh. "Why don't you go on back to Kansas City to your wife? I suppose she's the one you were talking to on the phone?"

"You suppose wrong." He smiled a mocking smile. "That happened to be a sweet young lady I met in Wichita last year. Perhaps it's time to head that way until my wife makes the right decision."

Tuck laughed. "I thought you were getting back together."

"Unfortunately, her father isn't quite ready to forgive me, and he controls the purse strings and his daughter." He bowed.

"Serves you right, you womanizing four-flusher." She spun and headed for the door.

His mocking laugh hit her like a sack of potatoes.

Boiling, seething anger roiled up inside her. Her hand clutched into a tight fist. Spinning around, she slammed her fist into his face.

He yelled and hit the floor.

With a tight smile, she rubbed her hands together. "Enjoy your trip."

She made it outside before her anger deflated, and she leaned against the front of the store, weak and trembling. How could she have been such a fool? He'd cared nothing for her. He had played with her affections and humiliated her. What kind of woman did he think she was that he would show disrespect to her so?

Batting tears from her eyes, she stalked over to the hitching rail. She mounted Sweet Pea and rode away toward the Collinses' farm. She had to talk to someone. She needed Rafe. He was the only one who could always help her think straight.

A pang shot through her, and she yanked on the reins, bringing Sweet Pea to a stop. How could she have forgotten? Things were different between her and Rafe now. He wasn't just her best friend anymore.

Shame washed over her at the very thought of revealing to him the things Sam had admitted to her. Oh, how could she have thought she was in love with such a vile man? If only she could go back and do things differently. But she couldn't. All she could do now was try to salvage some of her dignity and get on with her life.

At least she had Ma and Pa and Addy. She'd never tell her parents the truth about Sam. If he was really leaving, they wouldn't have to know how bad it really was. But she could talk to her sister. Addy would help her through this.

Suddenly she thought of Ma's favorite scripture verse. *"Commit thy works unto the Lord, and thy thoughts shall be established."* She'd never even consulted with God about Sam. She'd wanted her own way, and it had never crossed her mind to ask God if Sam was His will for her life.

"Father, forgive me for being so willful. From now on I only want to do things Your way. And Lord, I can't imagine my life without Rafe in it. But I know I'm the one who messed everything up. Really, I only need You. Please don't let Rafe be hurt because of me. Have Your way, Lord. In Jesus' name. Amen."

Peace flowed over her as she headed for home.

❧

"I tell you, Jim, if that guy hurts her, I don't know what I'll do."

Jim gave him a commiserating look and nodded. He'd come over to say good-bye before he left for Arkansas and had stayed for lunch.

Rafe leaned back in the chair and glanced out over the yard. The rain had picked up again, and there wouldn't likely be a leaf left on a tree if it kept up. They'd held on pretty long as it was, considering this was the third week in November. He threw the piece of wood he'd been chewing on into the yard. "Oh well, enough of my whining. I'm sorry to see you go, Jim."

"Thanks, Rafe, but now that Marble Cave is shut down for the winter, I need to go where the work is," Jim said.

"Too bad you won't be around for Thanksgiving. My ma's pumpkin pies are the best in the county." His mouth nearly watered just thinking about them.

"I hear you. She makes a real good turkey, too." He grinned. "Rafe, I wouldn't worry about Tuck if I were you. She's a smart girl and independent. She'll catch on to Fields sooner or later."

"Sooner I hope." Some women never found out their men were rotten, until they were wed and expecting babies. His stomach tightened at the thought of Tuck in a situation like that.

"Don't give up on her. She might care more about you than you think." Jim's voice held hope, and Rafe knew he was probably wishing the same about Addy, although he'd barely spoken ten words to her since the first time he laid eyes on her.

He sighed. "I don't know, Jim. When I came out of the barn last night after talking to her pa, she'd gone in the house. My horse was in plain sight, so she knew I was there. Didn't say hello or even ask me to help her carry the supplies in."

"Did you go in and say hello to her?" Jim gave him a knowing look.

"Nope. She'd have known something was wrong, and she has a way of wringing the truth out of me. I couldn't be the one to tell her, so I left."

"Well, she may have had her reasons for not coming to tell you hello." Jim didn't sound too convinced, much less convincing.

Rafe nodded. "Maybe."

"You sure you don't want to go with me to Arkansas? They're still needing hands. Maybe a change in scenery is what you need. It could help you think clearly." He snapped his fingers. "I almost forgot to tell you. I found out why they're buying up land all around the store and mill."

"Why?" Rafe turned his attention fully on what Jim was saying. Nearly everyone he'd talked to lately had wondered about that.

"Seems the Missouri Pacific plans on building a township. They'll keep the name of Branson, since that's what most people call the community already."

"Is that right? That's interesting," Rafe said. "Old man Berry might have something to say about that. You know he owns the land the store and post office are on. He's the one who wants the mail to be postmarked Lucia instead of Branson. I'd hate for that to happen, but who knows?"

Jim shook his head and stood. "The railroad will more than likely buy that property, too, so that'll take care of that."

"Yes. If Berry will sell. He's a hardworking, God-fearing man, but a stubborn old coot as well. If he decides not to sell, his sons will stand behind him. They're a close-knit bunch." Rafe stretched and stood up, reaching out to shake Jim's hand.

"Well, I'll be back this way in a few months, if not sooner. It'll depend on when Lynch wants to reopen." He mounted his horse. "Good-bye, Rafe."

"Good-bye and take care. Depending on what happens

here, I may follow you." He waved and headed for the barn as Jim rode away.

His pa was currying Paintbrush, the Indian pony they'd had since Rafe was a boy. Pa treated all his animals well, but Paintbrush was special. He got the finest care of any horse they'd ever owned.

"Pa, I found out why the railroad's buying up so much land. They plan on building a town over by Branson's."

"You don't say. What do they want with a town? Must be up to something." Pa scratched his ear and frowned, two deep lines appearing between his eyes.

"Or maybe they plan to bring some businesses in here." Excitement rose in Rafe, almost making him forget his worry about Tuck.

"Hmm. Well, I sure ain't selling. They'll get my farm over my dead body." Pa gave an emphatic nod and patted Paintbrush on the rump. "There you go, old feller. Pretty as can be and not a burr in sight."

"Well, I thought you'd want to know," Rafe said. "Is there anything I can do?"

"Yes, you can tell me why you been in such a bad mood all day. Your ma's right worried about you, boy."

Rafe cleared his throat before answering. "Sorry, Pa. I know I've been sort of moping around lately. I'm a little worried about Tuck and that doctor. I don't trust him to treat her right."

"Ain't no use worrying. When a gal takes a shine to a fellow, ain't nothing can get him out of her head unless something opens her eyes and she sees for herself." He turned slowly, rubbing his lower back. "But I don't blame you for not trusting that Fields fellow. I've thought he was a bad one ever since I laid eyes on him."

Rafe nodded. Maybe he needed to have a talk with Tuck after all. She couldn't do much more than bite his head off.

He took a deep breath. He couldn't do it. Not yet. Maybe Jack had spoken to her about it.

Pain stabbed at his heart as He walked to the house with his pa. He had to do something. If he couldn't talk to Tuck about it, there wasn't a thing to prevent him from talking to Sam Fields. Tomorrow he'd see the doctor again. This time he'd have a few questions for the man. If he didn't like the answers, he would talk to Tuck, even if she hated him for it.

sixteen

Tuck emitted a growl of frustration as Tom hit the wrong note on his banjo for about the tenth time since they'd started practicing, followed by an apologetic look at Mr. Willie. She frowned at all three of the men. "What's wrong with all of you today? Mr. Willie, your fiddle sounds like a dying cow and Squeezebox's accordion sounds like a dying bull. I can't even think of anything that sounds like Tom's banjo. Someone want to tell me what's going on?"

She was exaggerating, but so what? She knew what their problem was. And it was time to bring it to an end. "Look. It's not that I don't appreciate your concern, but I've told you over and over I'm all right. I don't care a hoot about Sam Fields hotfooting it out of here last night. I'd already ended things with him. The only thing I'm sorry about is that we won't have a doctor close by."

Tom gave her a look that wasn't quite disbelief but pretty close. "You sure, Tuck? Because every man in this town is willin' and ready to go after him and give him a trouncing if he just run off and left you, so to speak."

Tuck rolled her eyes and looked upward. "Mercy. What do I have to do to get it through your thick skulls?"

"How about you'uns leaves the girl alone?"

Bless Mr. Willie's heart. He always looked after her feelings. Tuck glanced around at her three friends. They'd known her since she was a little girl, and she had no doubt that each loved her in his own way. Why not tell them the truth?

She swallowed and sighed. "Well, I guess you might as well

know what's going on. But you have to promise you won't breathe a word of this to anyone because I'd be downright humiliated if it got around."

Squeezebox frowned. "You know we ain't loose-lipped, young lady. Tell us or not, don't make no never mind to me."

Tuck gave him a lopsided grin. "I know that. I'm just trying to get up the courage to tell you."

"Wal, just say it, gal." Tom's tone was much more gentle than usual.

"Sam Fields didn't just turn out to be a no-good skunk. He's a married, no-good skunk." She inhaled deeply and let the air out with a *whoosh*. There. She'd told. No one but Addy knew that bit of information. She hadn't even revealed it to Ma and Pa.

"Well, I'll be." Squeezebox's eyes widened. "Do you mean that so-called respectable doctor was a bigamist?"

Tom gave him a disgusted look. "He'd have to have married two women for him to be a bigamist. He's just a four-flushing womanizer. And I'd like to get my hands on him for deceiving our little gal here."

Tuck glanced at Mr. Willie, surprised that he hadn't said a word. Lips pressed tightly together and brow wrinkled, his eyes blazed. If she'd ever seen murder in anyone's eyes, she was seeing it now, in the countenance of the gentle, tenderhearted Willie Van Schultz. "Mr. Willie?" She laid a hand on his shoulder. "Please. I'm all right. I promise."

"He never laid nary a hand on you, did he?" The words were like bullets. She shuddered, wondering what he'd do if he knew about the night by the river.

"He never did." Mr. Willie didn't need to know how close that came to being a lie.

Mr. Willie nodded, and his face relaxed a little, but his eyes still smoldered.

Another shiver ran over Tuck. She knew little to nothing

about Mr. Willie's past, but she had a feeling ...it different from his present peaceful existence.

He sat up and positioned his fiddle. "Wal, we b... ...it dillydallyin' and get busy if we're going to be ready for the Christmas dance."

Tuck, relieved to have the subject over and hopefully done with, tucked her collar inside her dress and got ready to play. Maybe her life would get back to normal now. Her heart seemed to tilt. Except for her and Rafe. She shook her head to expel the thought. No time for that now.

After the practice, Tuck rode home to find the parlor filled with chattering ladies. She slapped herself on the forehead. She'd completely forgotten the ladies involved in the Christmas bazaar would be here for a final meeting. The bazaar was being held the first week in December, and there were always last-minute plans to cover.

Besides the bazaar, Tuck had to get music ready for the Christmas dance, and she had a dress to finish. She'd also need to help with baking for the holidays. Maybe she was spreading herself too thin. How could she be expected to remember everything? On the other hand, staying busy was probably good for her. At least it would help keep her mind off Rafe.

"Sorry, everyone." She smiled apologetically as she stepped into the parlor. "I was with the oldsters, practicing. I forgot all about the meeting."

"Abigail." Ma smiled a welcome. "How did your practice go?"

She walked over and kissed her ma on the cheek. "It was a good practice. Never fear, ladies. Our music will be ready for the dance."

Ma's Aunt Kate waved from across the room. "We're very grateful for your talent, Abigail, as well as the oldsters as you call them."

"Hummph." Mrs. Humphrey's eyes darted disapproval.

"Yes, and that sounds very disrespectful to me. Besides, in my opinion, she's much too familiar with those old men. Men being what they are."

"Mother!" Aletha Humphrey's whisper was loud enough to reach Tuck's ears. "Please don't start."

"Start? Start what? I guess I have a right to express my opinion."

"Well, I think Abby and the *oldsters* are perfectly delightful, and the friendship they all share is lovely." Mrs. Dobson, a friend of Aunt Kate's, smiled at Tuck. "And by the way, Abby, you worked very hard for the fall festival and dance. And now you're going to be playing for the Christmas dance as well. It's time you had some fun. I think you should leave this bazaar to us older women so you can enjoy it with the rest of the young folks."

Murmurs of assent greeted Mrs. Dobson's suggestion.

"Thank you, Mrs. Dobson. I believe I'll take you up on that." Tuck grinned. "Now may I serve you ladies tea or something?"

"We're about to finish up here, dear." Ma said. "We had our refreshments earlier."

"Then I think I'll go find my sister." She gave a wave and headed for the kitchen.

The bazaar was only a few days away. She and Addy and Rafe had always hung out together at these gatherings. Except when Addy sometimes deserted them to visit with the other girls. Could she get up the courage to talk to Rafe before then? She sighed. Probably not. It would very likely do her good to spend more time with the other girls her age anyway. Maybe she could learn something useful.

Of course, Rafe had indicated to her pa that he didn't like the change in her. But she was through trying to please men. She'd be herself. And there was nothing wrong with continuing to cultivate ladylike manners, even if she did still wear overalls.

Rafe hung onto the plow as the mules pulled the blade through Ma's depleted house garden. As soon as this plot was turned under, he'd be done with plowing until spring planting time. Then the long winter would drag on forever. Or so it seemed.

Ordinarily he'd be looking forward to the Christmas bazaar. Not because he liked it but because he and Tuck always had a lot of fun together. Not this year though. Tuck wasn't speaking to him.

He'd seen her over by the mill yesterday, and she'd turned and headed down to the river, pretending not to see him. Maybe she was embarrassed because the doc took off without a by-your-leave. Or maybe his company just wasn't to her liking any more.

Anger flashed through him. Who needed her anyway? She didn't even act like a girl half the time. Maybe he wasn't really in love with her but was just used to her. Like an old shoe. It was hard to let go.

He kicked at a clod of hard dirt then yelled across the field, "I don't need you, Tuck Sullivan. You're not the only fish in the ocean."

That's right. Lots of pretty little fish. Like Carrie Sue who wanted nothing better than to bat her pretty blue eyes at him. Maybe it was time to pay some close attention to those eyes. Of course no one had blue eyes like Tuck's. He kicked another dirt clod. He could forget her and he'd start right now.

After he'd eaten supper and done his evening chores, Rafe tidied up then saddled Champ. He belted out "Old Dan Tucker" at the top of his voice while he rode. By the time the Andersons' farm came into view, he was feeling a lot better. Maybe life had something to offer him after all.

He jumped off Champ and sauntered to the front door. After knocking, he stood, hat in hand, a big smile on his face.

Mrs. Anderson opened the door to his knock, and when she saw him, her eyes sparkled. "Good evening, Rafe. Won't you come in?"

Rafe wiped his feet on the pile of old rags outside the door and stepped inside. "Thank you, ma'am. Is Carrie Sue home by any chance?"

"She certainly is. Here, make yourself at home in the parlor and I'll go get her." She nearly skipped down the hall.

Rafe sat on an overstuffed sofa, twisting his hat in his hands, and waited what must have been at least thirty minutes. Fidgeting, his exuberance wore off little by little. This had been a mistake, a big mistake. Should he make an excuse and leave? He stood then plopped back down. Nope. The gossip would be all over the county, and when Ma heard it, she'd be humiliated and probably take a broom to him.

"Hello, Rafe." Carrie Sue stood in the doorway dressed for company. His company. Her blond tresses were swept back from her face, and her blue eyes shone.

Rafe stood. "Hello, Carrie."

"You wanted to see me?" Her voice cracked, and she blushed as she seated herself in a chair across from the sofa.

The blush and nervousness of her voice were his undoing. He couldn't back out now. She'd be hurt and insulted. On the other hand, he couldn't make small talk for an hour either. Smiling, he reclaimed his seat on the sofa. "I know it's rather late for an invitation to the bazaar, but if you haven't made other plans, would you like to go with me?"

Her face brightened, and a pretty pink blush washed over her smooth cheeks. "Why yes, I'd love to accompany you to the bazaar. Thank you for asking me."

"It's my pleasure." He stood and smiled down at her. "Well then, I'll come by around eleven. That way we can eat lunch before we look through the booths."

"That sounds wonderful. But. . .what about Tuck?" She

dropped her lashes then raised them slowly.

"What do you mean?" He raised an eyebrow.

"Oh, now that Dr. Fields is gone, I thought you two—" She broke off in apparent confusion.

Rafe tensed against the stab of pain but managed a laugh. "Tuck and I are just friends. I thought everyone knew that."

"Oh, that's wonderful. I mean. . .you and Tuck were always together before the doctor started courting her, so I assumed that you were in love with her." She lifted her chin, gazed at him with eyes that might have bowled him over if she hadn't just mentioned Tuck and fluttered her long lashes.

"In love with Tuck? Not at all." He gave a short laugh, but a sick feeling tugged at his stomach. "Well, I'll see you Saturday then."

A coquettish smile tipped her lips, and she nodded. "I'll look forward to it, Rafe."

He took the tiny hand she offered him and shook it gently, then swallowed past the lump in his throat.

She shut the door, and before he made it off the porch, he heard her scream of excitement. He grinned. She must like him more than he'd thought.

He whistled as he rode away on Champ. He patted the horse on the neck and crooned. "Yes, I think the girl was happy to see me, old boy."

He laughed. What would Tuck think when he showed up with Carrie Sue at his side? His stomach lurched. What if Tuck had been hiding away because she was hurting? He'd been so happy when he heard Fields had left, it hadn't occurred to him that Tuck might suffer. Maybe that's why she'd avoided him. She couldn't face anyone. She probably felt humiliated, too. He groaned. What had he done? He should have given her more time. Instead he'd just kept company with another woman and had even pretty well denied being in love with Tuck.

He pulled up on the reins. Champ gave an impatient whinny, then bent his head and munched at the brown grass. Maybe he should just go back and make some excuse to Carrie Sue. But it was too late for that. If word got around, which it would, he'd be branded as heartless, and some of the other females would laugh behind Carrie's back. He couldn't be the cause of that. That would be one step toward becoming a worthless sidewinder like Sam Fields.

seventeen

Tuck tapped her foot to a boisterous rendition of "Up on the House Top." In order to give Tuck and the oldsters a break, the Packard brothers, famous over the years for their leading of music at church socials and community parties, had come out of retirement for the occasion. She grinned as Horace, the eldest of the brothers, grabbed for the red stocking cap that had slipped from his balding head.

Wood smoke from the tall iron stove in the corner blended together with the fragrance of gigantic pine boughs that hung from the rafters of the Jenkinses' barn and the fronts of individual booths. Kettles emitted smells of cinnamon and clove.

Tuck inhaled deeply in appreciation. She smiled at the festive touch of holly berries and bright red bows trimmed in lace.

Addy smiled and waved at their friends, Phyllis and Jolene. "Let's go talk to them, Abby."

Tuck would just as soon not, but reminding herself she'd promised to spend more time with the other girls, she followed her sister without complaint. They stopped at one of the booths and purchased hot apple cider, then continued across the room.

"Oh, that cider smells delicious. I think I'll get a cup, too." Phyllis, her plump cheeks glowing, turned to Jolene. "Would you like me to bring something back to you?"

"I think I'll have cider, too. I can't resist it," Jolene said, her brown eyes sparkling. "Go to Thompson's booth. Mr. Thompson makes the best cider in the whole state."

Tuck grinned. Thompson's cider was good, but she suspected Jolene's love affair with it resulted from her crush on Ralph, the oldest Thompson son. The funny thing was Ralph had been moping after Addy and Tuck for years. He didn't seem to care which one.

Tuck glanced around for Rafe, having no idea what she'd do if she saw him. Memories of last year's bazaar assailed her mind, and longing washed over her. She missed him. There was no denying that. Would he seek her out when he got here? She didn't want that, did she?

"Why, look." Exaggerated surprise filled Jolene's voice. "There's my cousin, Carrie Sue. Isn't that Rafe beside her?"

With controlled calm, Tuck slowly turned her head. Rafe strolled past a quilt display, his attention on the girl at his side. Tuck clenched her teeth. Carrie Sue clung to his arm as though she was afraid he might get away. Which he would do, if he knew what was good for him. Carrie Sue certainly wasn't.

Phyllis gave Jolene a wry grin and tapped her on the arm. "As though you didn't know he was bringing her. You told me yesterday, silly."

Jolene had the grace to blush, accompanying it with a slight laugh. "Oh that's right. I forgot for a moment."

Tuck's breathing sped up then hitched when she tried to control it. *Oh God, please don't let me faint. I do want Rafe to be happy. If it was anyone but Carrie Sue. . .*

She started as her sister's breath warmed the skin by her ear. "Abby," Addy whispered, "pull yourself together. Don't give Jolene and Carrie Sue the satisfaction of knowing you care."

Tuck took a deep breath and gushed. "It *is* Rafe and Carrie Sue. How nice to finally see her with someone. She's been hunting for so long."

Oh, Rafe. It had only been a few days since she'd overheard him declare to Pa that he loved her. Had she misunderstood? She'd told herself at the time she wished only to be Rafe's friend. But seeing another woman at his side made a mockery of her words.

Jolene tossed her dark curls. "That was quite a rude thing to say, Abby. A number of young men have asked to court Carrie. I believe she's been saving herself for Rafe. I hope you have no problem with that."

Problem? She'd show her problems. Tuck opened her lips to lambast the girl who was supposed to be a friend, but a jerk on her arm brought her to her senses.

Addy smiled with warning in her eyes. "Come, Abby. Let's go look at the wood carvings. I believe some of Pa's are being presented." With another tug on Tuck's arm, she dragged her away.

They walked a few feet and stopped at a booth that featured a variety of Christmas themed linens.

"What did you do that for?" Tuck glared at her twin. "I didn't do anything."

"Abby," Addy spoke through clenched teeth, "you can't just fly off the handle at people whenever you feel like it."

"What? I didn't say a word." Tuck frowned.

"No, but you were about to, and don't deny it," Addy snapped.

"Well, talk about two peas in a pod. You girls even have twin frowns."

At the sound of Carrie Sue's voice, Tuck stiffened then whirled around. The simpering blond held onto Rafe's arm as though her life depended on it.

"Carrie Sue. Did anyone ever tell you your voice sounds like a screeching parrot?" Tuck inwardly cringed. Oh no. Did she really say that?

Addy gasped and glared at Tuck, then walked away, her face flaming.

Now she'd embarrassed Addy, and she probably wouldn't ever speak to her again.

Tuck glanced at Rafe and caught his mouth twisting and pressing together to hold back a grin. Whew. At least he wasn't mad at her for her unkind words. "Hi, Rafe."

"Hi, Tuck. Enjoying the bazaar?" His gaze bore into hers, and for once she couldn't read his eyes.

"Not much. You?" She deliberately ignored Carrie Sue, who stared daggers at her.

"Not re—" He glanced at Carrie and cleared his throat. "Sure. It's a great bazaar. We're just headed over to Thompson's booth to get some cider. Join us?"

Tuck almost laughed aloud at the exasperated sound that exploded from Carrie Sue. Rafe wasn't piling up a lot of points in his favor. He'd better watch it.

"Really, Rafe, I'm sure Abby has other things to do than tag along with us. Let's go."

Tuck toyed with the idea of hanging onto Rafe's other arm and going along just to aggravate Carrie Sue. But on second thought, she'd been rude enough for one encounter. Besides, Addy was furious enough with her already. If Rafe wanted to keep company with a silly thing like Carrie, he was welcome to her. She forced herself to smile. "No, thank you. I think I'll head outside for some fresh air. It's getting too stuffy in here for me."

Carrie Sue tossed her head and, with a pull on Rafe's arm, guided him away. He threw an unreadable glance over his shoulder at Tuck as he went, but with heaviness in her heart, she turned away.

She couldn't believe he would actually fall for Carrie Sue's silliness. Carrie was actually a nice girl, and she was very pretty with her shiny blond curls and enormous blue eyes. She'd always had a crush on Rafe. Furthermore, Tuck sighed as truth slammed into her thoughts. She'd probably make him a wonderful wife.

Pain shot through her gut and tightened her lips together. Rafe was hers. And she was his. That was the way it had always been. She just hadn't realized what it meant. Over her dead body would Carrie Sue or anyone else take him from her.

૨૦

Every time Rafe glanced at Tuck, his heart jumped like crazy and he couldn't stop smiling. Several times he'd caught her glancing at him and Carrie with jealousy all over her face. He'd always been able to read her like a book until Sam Fields came along. What better time for that ability to return?

A bubble of glee rose in him. Maybe she cared more about him than he realized. She might not even know it herself because she'd allowed infatuation for that doctor to cloud her reasoning. He didn't want to get his hopes up, but nevertheless, the possibility that he and Tuck had a chance seemed more certain than ever.

Carrie Sue returned his smile, her eyes shining with delight. It was obvious she believed she was the source of his happiness. Guilt wormed its way into his conscience. Carrie would be furious when she learned today was not only their first date but also their last. He didn't blame her. He should have never asked her to accompany him. Carrie was very nice and extremely pretty and would more than likely make some man a good wife. Just not him.

No other woman was as beautiful in his eyes as Tuck, with her wild curls and dancing eyes. And with the way she threatened to knock the tar out of him when he teased her.

A laugh escaped from his lips. Carrie glanced at him, and her joyous expression faded. She'd caught him staring at Tuck. Her face puckered, and she blinked back tears. She didn't deserve this. Guilt riddling him, Rafe reached out his hand to her. Shaking her head, she blinked back tears then composed her face. Relief mixed with his guilt. At least she wouldn't make a scene. Not in public at any rate.

Determined to avoid hurting Carrie as much as possible, he devoted himself to her for the rest of the afternoon, making a valiant, although not completely successful, attempt to keep his eyes off Tuck.

The bazaar shut down at six, and Rafe sighed a breath of relief as he helped Carrie Sue into the buggy. She appeared exhausted, perhaps from trying to keep up appearances. She'd done a good job so far. He just hoped she didn't tear into him on the way home, although it would serve him right if she did. She stiffened as he wrapped the carriage blanket around her to shield her from the cold night air.

The silence as they drove home only deepened Rafe's guilt. Carrie Sue deserved some sort of explanation or at least an apology. If he'd left her alone, she'd probably have spent this afternoon with someone who would have given her the admiration she deserved.

He cleared his throat, searching for the right words. "Carrie. . ."

"Never mind, Rafe. I know you love Abby. I've always known it. I guess when she started going out with the doctor, I hoped you would turn to me." She bit her lip then smiled. "It's all right. Don't worry, I won't go into seclusion. Several young men are waiting in line for my attention."

"I don't doubt that. You're a nice girl and very lovely, by the way." He smiled. "I thought you'd hit me over the head. Wouldn't blame you a bit if you did."

A sad smile tipped one side of her rosebud mouth. "You can't help who you love."

Rafe shook his head. That was another thing that puzzled him. He must really wear his heart on his sleeve. "How did you know I'm in love with Tuck? I didn't know myself until recently."

She laughed. "You two are so funny. Everyone knows you love each other. It's so obvious. How could we not know?"

"So you think Tuck loves me and doesn't know it?" He probably shouldn't be talking about loving Tuck with Carrie Sue, but he couldn't stop himself.

"I think she knows it now, Rafe. And if she doesn't realize you love her, she's blind as a bat."

Rafe turned into the Andersons' cedar-lined drive. When he stopped in front of the house, he took her hand. "Carrie Sue, if I wasn't so much in love with Tuck, I can't think of another girl I'd rather fall in love with than you."

"Pity's sake, Rafe. Stop trying to make me feel better. I'm quite all right. You're not the only eligible man in the county, you know." She laughed and tapped him on the arm. "You're not even the best-looking one."

Heat rose up his neck and singed his cheeks. Had he been assuming she cared more about him than she did? He must have sounded like an idiot.

"Oh, now I've embarrassed you." She patted his arm. "Sorry. Now help me down and go say sweet things to Abby. I'd say she's the one who'll hit you."

He wouldn't mind a pounding from Tuck about now. It wouldn't be the first time. Always in fun, of course. He chuckled. "You're more than likely right about that." He stepped out of the carriage and went around to help her out, then walked her to the door where she stopped.

"I wish I could say it was a wonderful afternoon, Rafe, but that wouldn't be exactly the truth, so I'll just say good-bye. I hope everything works out for you and Abby." She smiled and, with a little wave, opened the door and went inside.

Rafe breathed a sigh of relief that Carrie had been such a good sport and that he hadn't had to face her mother.

Night came early in Missouri this time of the year. The dark canopy above him as he drove away from the Anderson farm was studded with diamonds. Never had he seen such a night sky. He breathed in the clean night air then shivered from the coldness in his lungs. Tuck should be here with him. They'd always loved to go riding at night. Usually on horseback.

A picture of her astride Sweet Pea, her head thrown back in laughter, filled his thoughts, and his heart raced. What should he do now? He didn't want to make a wrong move and mess things up.

He'd see her at church in the morning. Maybe he could manage an invitation to dinner. Nah. He might have before, but things were different now. Maybe he'd invite her to dinner.

He sighed. The best thing would be to pray and leave it in God's hands. God would show him what to do. And Rafe would sure keep his eyes open so he wouldn't miss it.

eighteen

"Move over, Bessie. You're going to knock the bucket over." Tuck gave the cow's rump a shove then returned to the milking. Streams of milk dinging against the galvanized bucket combined with her daydreaming had almost caused her to doze off. Ma wouldn't have been happy, to say the least, if she'd lost all the milk due to carelessness. Nevertheless, Tuck couldn't keep the daydreaming at bay.

The memory of Carrie Sue hanging all over Rafe had tormented her ever since the bazaar, nearly a week ago. Every time the picture crossed her thoughts, a fresh pang sliced through her. She'd just begun to get used to the idea that Rafe was in love with her. Now he'd apparently forgotten his own feelings. Or, more likely, she had misunderstood what he said. If so, that was good. She and Rafe could go back to the way things used to be. Yes, that was good. But why didn't she feel like it was good?

"Abby, are you about done? It's getting colder." A gust of wind followed her twin through the barn door. Addy carried the egg basket in the crook of her arm. "Hurry and we can walk back to the house together."

That meant Addy wanted to question her again about how she felt about Rafe and Carrie Sue. The nosy thing. She'd been trying to get her to talk about it all week. Tuck didn't intend to utter one word about it.

"I'm not done with the milking yet. You go on. I'll be there in a few minutes." Maybe after she strained the milk she'd slip away and saddle Sweet Pea up for a ride.

"Oh, I'm in no hurry." Addy sat on a bale of hay with her

basket on her knees. "Wasn't the bazaar fun? We should have them more often. I loved the little wooden stars I bought for the Christmas tree."

"They are pretty. Did you show them to Ma?" Ma and Pa both loved Christmas. Tuck loved seeing Ma's childlike enthusiasm for the holiday.

"No, I want to keep them a secret until we get the tree." Addy loved decorating, but it fell to Pa and Tuck to fetch the evergreen every year.

"I can't believe it's only two weeks until Christmas." She supposed Rafe would spend the day with Carrie Sue. She took a deep breath and shoved the thought away. This was getting ridiculous.

Bessie mooed. Tuck started and stared at the bucket of milk.

"Abby, you haven't gotten a drop of milk in the past two minutes. What's wrong with you?"

Tuck sighed and stood, shoving the stool away with her foot. "Nothing. I guess I'm just still half asleep."

Addy stood. "Well, hurry and get Bessie back into her stall. I'm getting cold. Besides, we promised Ma we'd finish sewing our Christmas dresses today. The Christmas dance is only one week away."

"And one day." Tuck led Bessie back to her stall and forked some hay into her trough. Then, carrying the bucket of milk, she followed her sister out the door. Addy was right. The air felt a lot colder than when they'd come outside to do their morning chores.

Tuck washed her hands and strained the milk, then went to join Addy and Ma in the parlor for a long day of sewing. She wrinkled her nose at the thought. If she could afford it, she'd buy all her dresses ready-made.

Ma's smile didn't quite meet her eyes as she held out Tuck's gown with both hands. "Yours is all finished except for hemming."

"What? How?" She took the silky blue gown and held it up. Sure enough. The lace was even sewn on. "I haven't worked on it at all this week." Oops. She really needed to watch her words.

She cut a glance at Ma who was already busy arranging the piles of fabric in her lap.

"Addy did it for you." Ma glanced up and her eyebrows rose slightly. "In spite of her own work load."

Tuck flashed a quick glance of gratitude at Addy but wished her sister had been a little more secretive about the good deed. "Thanks, sis."

"It was no problem. You know I love to sew, and you've been busy practicing your music for the dance."

Tuck nodded. Addy was always taking care of her. She guessed it was a good thing.

Ma glanced up. "Yes, you do make beautiful music, Tuck. It was a blessing that Mr. Van Schultz was willing to take you under his wing."

"And Pap Sanders," Tuck said. "Don't forget Pap. If not for him, I might never have known I loved the fiddle."

She often thought back with nostalgia to those days when Papa Jack had been a riverboat captain. It was on the *Julia Dawn*, his boat, that Tuck and Addy had become fast friends with Pap Sanders, his fiddle-playing cook. When the old man had noticed Tuck's interest in the fiddle, he had taken her under his wing and taught her the basics. She'd done so well that Addy had insisted she take possession of their grandfather's violin. She sighed and stabbed her needle at the hem in her hand. The locket that lay beneath her shirt felt cold and heavy.

"Of course, Abigail," Ma's voice was tender. "I know Mr. Sanders played a large part in getting you started."

Tuck swallowed past a lump that had suddenly formed in her throat. Addy was always doing things on impulse to make Tuck feel better. She should never have allowed her sister to give her their mother's locket. It was precious to her, in a deep way it had never been to Tuck. Tuck had chosen the violin and would have done the same today.

Ma cleared her throat. "I wonder how Rafe is. I haven't seen him since the bazaar. The Anderson girl seems quite taken with him."

At the sudden turn in the conversation, Tuck jerked her head up and looked at Ma. She sat looking intently at her sewing, but Tuck wasn't fooled. Ma had always had a soft spot for Rafe and had even tried matchmaking a few times over the years. Huh. If she was trying to get a reaction out of Tuck, she was doomed to failure.

Still, it wouldn't hurt to take a ride over to Rafe's just to check out his intentions toward Carrie Sue. That is if she ever got this fool hem done.

❧

Rafe mentally patted himself on the back for coming up with the perfect Christmas present for his nephew, Bobby. Every time Rafe dropped by his sister Betty's house, the four-year-old plied him with questions about the White River Line. Just last week, Bobby had informed him that he wanted to be a train engineer when he grew up.

Rafe leaned back on the crate where he was sitting and examined the wooden train engine on the floor in front of him. It was shaping up nicely. All Rafe had to do now was attach the wheels and slap on a coat or two of paint. He could envision Bobby scooting around the house on it on Christmas day making train sounds.

At the sound of horse's hooves in the yard, Rafe got up and walked to the barn door. His heart jumped as Tuck slid off Sweet Pea and stepped up onto the porch. "Hey, Tuck," he yelled. "I'm out here."

She turned and waved, grinning as she walked toward him.

"Maybe I came to see your ma." She stopped in front of him. "Ever think of that?"

"Oh well, in that case, you'll find Ma in the house." He turned as though to walk away, then turned back around and grinned. "It's good to see you."

"You just saw me at the bazaar a few days ago," she retorted.

"You know what I mean."

"I know." She paused then shrugged. "I've missed you, too."

That sounded promising. If she meant it the way he hoped she did. He squinted at her. "I'm not the one that made myself scarce."

She stiffened, then relaxed and took a deep breath. "I know. Sorry about that, Rafe. I guess I went a little crazy over that no-good doctor."

He wouldn't exactly say she sounded hangdog, but accompanied by the regret in her voice, he knew she was beating herself up. "Hey, let's go fishing tomorrow." He cringed inwardly. That was brilliant.

She laughed. "If it keeps getting colder, the river will be iced over by then. At least part of it. What do you plan? Ice fishing?"

"Okay, okay. Bad idea. I have another one. That railroad guy is holding a meeting at the church house tomorrow. Want to go?" Not as good as fishing, but it could be interesting. At least he'd be spending time with Tuck.

She frowned. "What's going on with them? Do you know? I heard they're trying to buy up everyone's land."

"I'm not sure. Jim said they just want the area around Branson's and the mill."

Her eyes brightened. "Okay, we might as well go find out what they're up to. What time?"

"Ten o'clock, I think. If I hear differently, I'll ride over and let you know." He didn't really care what they did, so long as he could be with her. "Maybe you should mention it to your folks. My pa's going."

"I was thinking the same thing. They might want to attend the meeting." She glanced toward Bobby's train. "That's a nice train engine."

"Thanks. I'm making it for Bobby for Christmas." He eyed it. "Think he'll like it?"

"Will he be able to ride on it?" she asked.

"Yes, I'm getting ready to put the wheels on. It'll roll with a push of his feet, I hope. It's supposed to anyway."

Rafe had missed hearing her laughter, which rippled out now. "I'm sure it will. And yes, I think he'll love it. What little boy wouldn't?"

"I would've," he said.

"Sure, you'd have loved taking it apart." She cut a sarcastic glance his way.

"Now what makes you say that?" he asked with a chuckle.

"As if you didn't know. Remember the time you took Hank's desk apart?"

"Well, a screw was in crooked. How was I to know the whole thing would fall apart?"

"Ha. Only after you removed about a dozen more of them." She bent over with laughter.

The next thing he knew they were both howling.

Tuck wiped her sleeve across her eyes. Was she crying? If so, he understood. Even if she never loved him the way he wanted her to, at least they hadn't lost what they had before. He hadn't lost his best friend.

Emotion welled up in him, and he swallowed hard. "You want to help me paint this thing, after I get the wheels on?" He immediately regretted the invitation. The first, last, and only time they'd painted anything together, she'd made such a mess he'd had to do the whole job over.

She laughed. "You should see your face. Don't worry. I'm not taking you up on that."

He blew out an exaggerated sigh of relief. "Well then,

we can go inside and beg Ma for some of those Christmas cookies she's been hiding for the last week."

"I'd love to, but I need to get home. I sort of sneaked out when no one was looking, and we're baking today, too." She smiled. "I'll see you in the morning then."

"Okay. . .uh. . .don't saddle Sweet Pea. I'll bring the buggy." Warmth spread across his face.

She blinked, and pink washed over her face. Was that a blush or a flush or anger? She blinked again. Her lips tipped at one corner. Was she going to yell? "Okay, that would be nice. See you then." She mounted Sweet Pea and rode away without a glance back.

Delight rushed over Rafe, and he couldn't keep from grinning. Tuck cared. He knew she did. The question was did she know it?

"Waaaaahooooo." His cry of victory resounded across the yard. The hound jumped up and bayed. Rafe threw his head back and laughed.

He'd have to go slowly. But not too slowly. He wasn't about to take any chances on losing Tuck when he was this close to winning her.

nineteen

A nervous murmur rippled throughout the packed church. Tuck sat with Rafe on the bench beside his parents. His brother-in-law, Robert, sat at the other end. Ma, Pa, Addy, and Aunt Kate were in front of them.

Fullbright, the railroad representative, stepped up on the platform and stood behind the pulpit. He cleared his throat and glanced down at some papers before him on the pulpit. "Ladies and gentlemen, thank you for coming." His voice boomed across the room. At least they'd be able to hear him.

Tuck forced herself to sit straight while Rafe leaned forward, his arms crossed on the back of the bench in front of them, his eyes focused on the railroad man.

"First of all, let me introduce myself. My name is Charles Fullbright. As most of you probably know, I'm an employee of the Missouri Pacific Railroad, and yes, I'm here to obtain land."

"You're not getting mine." Howard Thompson, who owned a small farm a few miles away, stood and shook a fist toward Fullbright. Another, then another, joined him, their angry voices added to his.

Fullbright raised his hand and shouted. "We don't want your farmland."

The men sat down, but uncertainty, if not downright disbelief, remained on their faces.

"Let me explain. I'm sure every one of you is aware of the Missouri Pacific's plans to build a line following the White River, from Helena, Arkansas, to Carthage, Missouri. The White River Line will not only benefit the railroad but

148

everyone who lives along the line."

Heads bobbed in agreement, but Thompson shouted, "What does that have to do with your buying land around here?"

"That's a legitimate question. One I'm happy to answer. The White River Line, although beneficial to all, will be very expensive to construct." He paused, but now he had their attention and no one spoke.

"My assignment here is to purchase land around and near the post office. This land will, in turn, be sold for businesses. In this way, the White River Line will be funded, and the Branson Town Company will create opportunities for progress in the community. We hope to plant orchards along the line as well, and encourage new mining ventures. All our plans will be beneficial to you. As many of you know, we have already obtained a great deal of land uphill from the river, but we need more."

As Fullbright paused, excited chatter broke out.

Rafe sat back and grinned at Tuck. "Looks like we're going to have a real town. Branson, Missouri."

"Just a minute." The loud voice cut through the noise. Tuck turned to see Thomas Berry, the old man who owned the land on which the store and post office were built. He swayed as he stood. Tuck thought for a moment he might fall. "There's one problem with your plan. I'm not selling my land to you or anyone else. In fact, I have plans to plat a town of my own, the town of Lucia, Missouri. From now on all mail leaving from the post office on my land will be marked Lucia, not Branson. So you may as well take your men and find another post office to build your town around." He turned and stomped out, followed by his son.

"I had a feeling." Pa muttered with a sigh. "I thought Berry would put the brakes on this."

"Well, that was interesting." With a little laugh, Mr. Fullbright took charge of the meeting once more. "I can assure you, Branson Town will be platted. With or without Mr. Berry's land. Now I'll open the meeting to questions and discussion."

The meeting lasted for another hour as Fullbright attempted to avert any concerns the people had. Rafe listened closely and even asked a couple of questions. Tuck's concentration had shifted from Fullbright. She couldn't get Mr. Berry off her mind.

By the time they came out of the stuffy church building, Tuck was more than ready to breathe some fresh air. Even cold air. After waving good-bye to Ma, Pa, and Addy, she let Rafe help her into his buggy.

They drove away from the church, and Rafe headed down the river road. He glanced at Tuck with a grin. "Branson, Missouri. Has a nice sound, doesn't it?"

"Yes, it does. I like it a lot better than Lucia. But what if Mr. Berry won't sell?"

"I don't think you need to worry about that." Rafe chuckled. "This is the railroad, remember? They usually get what they want."

Tuck bit her lip. "Why can't they start a town without the post office?"

He shook his head. "It wouldn't work."

"It doesn't seem quite right, does it?" She chewed on her bottom lip.

"What doesn't sound right, honey?" He looked at her with interest.

Tuck's stomach leaped at the endearment, and for a moment she couldn't speak. She took a deep breath. "Well, shouldn't a man be able to keep his land if he wants to?"

Rafe frowned. "Well yes, but sometimes there are exceptions. By holding out like he wants to do, he's preventing us from having a town."

"He says he wants to plant a town himself," Tuck snapped.

"What's wrong with that? Why shouldn't he? What gives the railroad any right to come in and take over?"

Rafe was quiet for a moment. "Tuck, we need the railroad. Without it, our progress is pretty much at a standstill."

She nodded but didn't reply. She could see both sides, but Mr. Berry had fought in the Civil War. He'd worked hard farming and doing blacksmith work for the community. He had a very large family. Why shouldn't he be able to leave them the land they'd been born on?

"Hey, Tuck. Let's go grab something to eat at my house then go hunting. You haven't gone with me a single time this season," His eyes sparkled as he smiled at her.

Oh, how she'd missed his smile, the fun in his eyes. "I'll have to go change. I can't go hunting in a dress."

"We're almost to my place. Why go all the way back? You can wear something of mine. Ma won't care."

Scandalized, Tuck stared at him with wide eyes. Although they really weren't any different than her own overalls, still, the idea of wearing a pair of pants that Rafe had worn sent heat rushing over her face and down her chest. "Why, Rafe Collins, shame on you. I can't wear your clothes."

His face turned red. "Okay, okay, we'll go back. Don't get so upset." He turned the horse and they headed back.

Surprised, she stared at him. She'd never seen Rafe give in so easily before.

⁂

Rafe stuck his tongue in his cheek as he crept through the trees. He didn't expect to kill anything with all the noise he and Tuck were making from their laughter and cutting up, but who cared?

They'd spent the whole morning and half the afternoon together. After his initial embarrassment at Tuck's reaction to his offer had worn off, he was just plain tickled. It was the first sign he'd had that she was thinking of him as a man instead of a childhood friend.

That wasn't the only thing different. Although it had bothered him to see her changing for Sam Fields, he had to admit, now that she had discarded the silliness, he didn't mind some of the more feminine characteristics she'd picked up from Addy. Obviously they were already a part of her and had just needed to be brought out. Otherwise, they'd have dropped away like some of the silly stuff had done as soon as Fields was out of the picture. Not that he wouldn't have been just as happy if she'd gone completely back to her old ways. She was Tuck. His Tuck. He loved the person she was.

He'd kept up a continuous line of humor going for hours just so he could hear her laugh.

Now, she walked close beside him, her rifle lying casually in the crook of her arm. "Rafe, we haven't spotted anything, and I'm tired of walking through these woods. We've been off your property for the last two hours. Maybe we'd better start back."

"I've got a better idea. Let's start a fire and talk some more. It won't be dark for a while yet."

"Sounds good. Lead the way."

After another half-hour's hike, they forged their way from the thick wooded area into a clearing. A cedar-grown hill rose on one side.

"Willie's cabin is around here somewhere. Maybe we could search for it and surprise him."

"Nah. We could wander around for two days before we found it." Besides, Rafe wanted to be alone with Tuck. He planned to let her know how he felt about her before the day was over.

"Is the wind picking up?" She shivered as she helped Rafe gather small pieces of wood to get a fire started.

"Maybe a little. You'll warm up as soon as that wood catches good." He grabbed a bigger piece of wood and threw it on with the others.

As the fire caught, they continued to pile on branches and fallen logs until they had a small-sized but roaring bonfire.

Tuck sat on the ground and leaned back on her elbows, her legs stretched toward the fire.

Rafe dropped down beside her. Her half-closed eyes caused Rafe's breath to catch in his throat. He let it out with a *whoosh*. He'd never thought of Tuck as sultry before. His hand trembled as he put another dead log on the fire. "That fire feels good, doesn't it?"

"Hmmm." She sat up and rubbed her arms. "Not really. Is it getting colder? I'm freezing."

"You really are cold, aren't you?" He put his arm around her and pulled her close, tucking her head beneath his chin. "Let's warm up some then head back toward the house so I can take you home."

"Carrie Sue might not like it if she saw you hugging me like this, you know. She might not understand that we're just friends."

He grinned, trying not to laugh. He'd been waiting for her to bring up Carrie Sue, as he knew she would, sooner or later, if she really cared about him. "I imagine she'd think I was in love with you."

Tuck emitted a not very convincing chuckle. "The silly girl."

"Actually, she's a very nice girl. Not nearly as silly as she seems." He hugged her a little closer. Warmth wrapped him in a pleasant cocoon, and he doubted the fire had much to do with it.

"That's nice. She's very pretty, too." Her voice tensed.

"Oh yes, very pretty." Laughter threatened to spring up from the joy in his heart.

She lifted her head and took a deep breath. "I suppose she'll make a good wife."

He shoved her head back down. "Yes, I'm sure she will."

She grew very still. He could barely make out her words, she spoke so quietly. "So when are you getting married?"

"Just as soon as I can." He wondered how long it would take her to catch on.

"Well, have you set a date yet?" She shot the words through clenched teeth.

"No." He grinned. "I thought I'd leave that up to you."

"What?" She sat up and stared at him.

"Hey, what's going on down there?" The yell came from up the hill.

Tuck shoved away from Rafe and jumped up.

Rafe groaned. Things had been going so well, too. In another moment he'd have asked her to marry him. Served him right for teasing her. He stood and peered up the hill.

Willie Van Schultz was making his way down the brushy path. "Well, I'll be. You two don't have any sense at all. Can't you see a storm's on the way?"

Rafe glanced up at the sky. Why hadn't he noticed the heavy gray clouds? "Looks like we're in for some snow."

"A lot of it, from the look of that sky. The way the wind's blowing, it may turn into a blizzard, too." He eyed them and their rifles. "Don't reckon you rode your horses. Come on. My cabin's just over the hill. I'll take you home."

Tuck mumbled something about not realizing his cabin was that close. Rafe sent her a worried look. Her face was ashen.

After they'd extinguished the fire, Tuck followed Willie up the hill with Rafe trailing behind. Ever since Willie had shown up, she'd avoided Rafe's eyes and hadn't spoken a word directly to him.

He had to find a way to talk with her privately. She had no idea that he'd been teasing her, and from the conversation they'd had, she must think he was in love with Carrie Sue and planned to marry her. Now how was he going to get out of this crazy situation?

twenty

Mr. Willie, usually quiet, sang Christmas carols nearly all the way. After church last Sunday, Ma had invited him, along with Tom and Squeezebox, to share their Christmas dinner, since none of the oldsters had family nearby. This had become a tradition the last few years, and Mr. Willie looked forward to it. Tuck was relieved she didn't have to talk.

For some reason, Rafe had lost the good mood he'd been in earlier. Probably wishing he was with Carrie Sue instead of Tuck and Mr. Willie.

Sleet began to fall as Mr. Willie turned off the river road and headed toward the Sulllivan farm. "I reckon this here is one of the nicest pieces of land in the county. Yore pa's done a right good job of improving it, too."

Tuck forced a smile on her numb lips. She'd been strangely numb since Rafe had dropped his news on her. Of course, he couldn't know how it affected her. To Rafe, she was a pal, nothing more.

When they stopped at her front steps, she jumped out and waved at them both. Rafe gave her a strangely desperate look as Mr. Willie drove away. Tuck slunk inside, wishing there was some way to avoid the family. They'd know something was wrong, and she'd have to tell them. Their sympathy would make the pain worse.

The house was silent. A note from Addy lay on the kitchen table stating that Pa was driving her and Ma to town to get some more baking supplies. Tuck breathed a sigh of relief and went to her bedroom.

She threw a log on the smoldering fire and dropped into

one of the rocking chairs. How could she have been so foolish? She'd wasted months running after a no-good man, and in the process, she'd lost Rafe, her best friend, and she now admitted to herself, much more than a friend. If there was such a thing as soul mates, she and Rafe fit the picture.

She must have misunderstood when she thought he'd told Pa he loved her. He couldn't have fallen out of love with her and in love with someone else that quickly. But even so, the old camaraderie was still there. Being with Rafe today had been like coming home. That was until he told her he was going to wed Carrie Sue. A surge of pain shot through her, and she jumped up and paced the floor, finally stopping at the wardrobe that held the new dresses.

Her blue gown hung next to Addy's rose-colored one. She brushed a finger across the delicate lace on the scooped collar. Would Rafe think it was pretty? He probably wouldn't even notice. He'd be too busy looking at Carrie.

She spun around and paced to the window then back. A picture of Carrie floating across the dance floor in Rafe's arms assaulted her imagination. A sob tore at her throat. She hated Carrie. She wished she'd die. Tuck groaned. She fell into her chair and let the tears flow.

God, I'm so sorry. I don't really hate her. It just hurts so much. Help me to bear it.

The door opened and closed, and then Addy's soft hand brushed Tuck's hair back. "Abby, what's wrong?"

Oh no. She hadn't heard the wagon drive up. But it was Addy, and Addy always made everything better.

Tuck flung herself around and into her sister's arms. "Rafe's going to marry Carrie Sue."

"What? No, he isn't," Addy said. She drew back and lifted Tuck's chin. "Where did you get an idea like that?"

"He told me so himself. It's true. I've lost him, and it's all my fault." She broke out in a fresh barrage of tears.

"What? But Tuck, it can't be true." Addy held Tuck and patted her while she continued to cry.

"Why can't it be true?" Tuck sat up and fisted her eyes, gulping back tears. "People fall in love every day and get married. Why shouldn't Rafe?"

"Of course Rafe should get married. But not to Carrie Sue." Confusion crossed her face, and bewilderment filled her voice.

"Why not to Carrie Sue? She doesn't exactly look like a horse, you know."

Addy pulled back and stared at her. "No, but—"

Tuck should do something for Carrie. She gasped. Was that thought from God? It must be. But could she bring herself to do anything for Carrie Sue? Maybe not, but she could do it for Rafe. Yes, she'd do it for Rafe. Then no one would know her heart was breaking.

"Addy, I'm going to ask Carrie what I can do to help her plan the wedding. I can do that much for Rafe. If I'm a friend to Carrie Sue, maybe she at least won't make him hate me." She choked back a sob. "Maybe I can even see him now and then."

Addy's hands grabbed her shoulders and shook. "Abby, listen to me. It's not true. I saw Carrie at the store today, and she was prattling along all excited about the dance. She's going with Frank Cade."

"Huh?" She tried to make sense of her sister's words.

"Yes. She said Rafe is obviously head over heels in love with you. Then she said if you have any sense, you'll grab him before he finds out what you're really like." Addy paused and, obviously realizing she shouldn't have revealed that, blushed a bright pink. "I told her that wasn't very nice, and she just laughed and said she doesn't care a bit and intends to get on with her life."

"But. . ." Tuck let her mind wander back over her conversation with Rafe while they sat by the bonfire. What exactly had he said? He said Carrie was nice. Then he agreed that she was pretty. Then when Tuck said she'd make a good wife, he said he was sure she would. Then Tuck had asked when they. . .no, when he was getting married. And he said—

She gasped. A smile tried to peek out from her tear-ravaged face. Joy and anger battled.

"That dirty dog! I'm going to kill him."

"Now, calm down, Abby. You know Rafe can't resist a good joke. And you've really raked him over the coals these last few months because of your infatuation with Sam."

"Well, that's not my fault!" She stopped. Of course it was her fault. "Oh, I don't care. He flat deceived me, and he did it on purpose. And here I've been bawling like a three-year-old. You just wait until I see him."

※

The ax blade whizzed the air and hit the short log, splitting it down the middle. Rafe kicked the two halves aside and grabbed another log. Splitting wood was the best thing he knew to get rid of a case of nerves. And he had a bad one.

The sleet had changed to snow, and wind howled and beat against the house and against Rafe. It promised to be a bad storm, so even with the woodpile stacked high, the storm gave him an excuse.

He'd had no chance to explain to Tuck that he'd been teasing her about Carrie. Rafe had suggested that Mr. Willie take him and Tuck to his house and he'd drive her home, but Tuck had said no, she'd rather be dropped off first. If he could talk to her and get the Carrie Sue thing straightened out, all would be fine. He was 99 percent sure Tuck would accept his proposal and they could set a wedding date.

He figured after that everything would sort of work itself out. Pa'd already promised to deed enough land to him for a house and a little acreage. They'd need room for a garden and space for kids to run and play. Hope rose in him as his thoughts progressed.

He propped the ax upright on the ground and grinned, hardly noticing the flakes that pummeled him from all sides. He'd bet his and Tuck's kids would be a sight. He hoped they all had shocks of wild blond hair like Tuck. He picked up the ax and swung. Of course, he'd have to wait until after the winter to build, but they could live here with Ma and Pa until then. Tuck was already like one of their own.

Yep, he had it all figured out. The only problem was he couldn't leave the farm. Pa was down with flu, and Rafe had to take care of all the night chores as well as preparing the house and animals for a possible blizzard. The milking and feeding were already done, but by the time supper was over, it would be too late to go calling on anyone, even if the storm slacked up.

In the meantime, with Tuck thinking he was going to marry Carrie Sue, there was no telling what could go wrong. He'd just have to get over there first thing in the morning if the storm had died down and the snow wasn't too deep. Tuck'd be madder than an old wet hen when she found out he'd been teasing her, but she'd calm down after a bit. Just so she didn't run into Carrie Sue or one of her friends before Rafe could talk to her.

"Rafe!" He turned at his ma's call. She stood in the doorway, a shawl pulled tightly around her head and shoulders, her apron flapping in the wind. "You're scattering wood all over the yard. You'd best get it picked up and stacked on the woodpile before the snowstorm gets any worse. Supper'll be ready by the time you get it done."

"All right, Ma. I can taste those beans and fried potatoes now." He flashed her a smile.

At his words, her face brightened. "I've got biscuits in the oven, too. Your pa had a hankering for them." She smiled and slipped back inside.

Rafe's stomach rumbled. Some folks liked corn bread best, but Rafe didn't think anything was better with pinto beans than hot buttered biscuits. The tantalizing smell of beans simmering and potatoes frying in the old iron skillet lingered even with the door closed.

He wondered if Tuck made good biscuits. He was pretty sure she did. After all, Lexie was one of the best cooks around Branson, and she would have taught the girls.

His thoughts went to Addy. How would she feel about Tuck getting married and leaving home? For that matter, how would Tuck handle being away from her twin? They'd never been apart. Not even for one whole day and night. Rafe frowned. Well, if they got to missing each other too much, Addy could come live with her sister and him.

He chuckled as he placed the fresh split wood on the woodpile. He already had their lives worked out, and Tuck still thought he was marrying Carrie Sue.

After supper, Rafe looked in on his pa. He was sitting up in bed drinking a cup of coffee. Pa didn't drink much of the bitter liquid, but he had to have his hot, black coffee at breakfast and another right after the supper meal.

"Got the cows in the barn, son?" Pa wasn't used to being still, and Rafe had a feeling Ma wouldn't be able to keep him down for long.

"Yes, sir. Milking's done, all the stock's fed, and the chickens are shut up in the shed."

Pa nodded. "Good. Sorry you had it all to do by yourself."

Rafe shrugged. "No problem. How are you feeling?"

"Fit as a fiddle. I'll be up and about tomorrow." He peered at Rafe. "You got something on your mind, son?"

Rafe grinned. "I was wondering, as soon as you're up to it, if we could go check out my land. I thought maybe you could help me decide on the best spot for a house and barn."

"I reckon so. Any special reason you're in such a hurry?"

Rafe nodded. "I plan to ask Tuck to marry me."

"Is that right? Well that don't surprise me. I've always sort of expected it. Then that doctor showed up." He shook his head. "Guess she's over that."

"She was only infatuated. Nothing serious. Maybe it took something like that to wake me up to my true feelings," Rafe said. "You think it'll be all right for Tuck and me to move in here until I get a house built next spring?"

"Fine with me. But your ma's going to have a fit if you don't give her time to fix things up for your bride." He grinned. "You seem pretty all-fired sure Tuck's going to say yes."

Rafe stared at his pa. His mouth went dry and he licked his lips. Pa was right. He'd been living in a dream world for the past few hours, making all these plans, never once thinking Tuck might say no. And even if she said yes, she'd want time to make plans.

His expectancy deflated. What had he been thinking? He hadn't even asked to court her yet. He'd just taken it for granted because she acted a little jealous that she felt the same way he did. Maybe she was jealous because she didn't want to share his friendship. Carrie Sue's thinking Tuck was in love with him didn't make it so. Neither did his own wishful thinking.

He sighed. Maybe he'd better hold off on his plans for a while. He'd feel an awful fool if she laughed in his face.

twenty-one

"Abby, the dough is kneaded more than enough."

Tuck frowned at her sister and pounded her fist into the pillowy mass twice more. "Fine. You finish."

"Abby, come back here."

Ignoring Addy's imploring voice, Tuck headed to the parlor and looked out the window again. Would it ever stop? Drifts piled up high on the porch, and a vast carpet of snow stretched out as far as her eye could see. Four days of almost continuous snow was bad enough, but the howling wind made it impossible to even think clearly.

Pa made the arduous trip to the barn twice a day to tend to the animals, and Ma paced the floor each time until he was safely back inside. Tuck had pleaded with him to let her help, but he wouldn't hear of it.

At least the enforced confinement had calmed her temper down. She wasn't sure what kind of scene she'd have thrown if she'd seen Rafe anytime soon after hearing about his little joke on her. She still inwardly seethed over it, but at least she didn't want to tear his hair out by the roots.

She'd made Addy repeat Carrie Sue's words over and over until she had them memorized. If the girl was correct and Rafe truly was in love with Tuck, then he may have been trying to find out her feelings for him, and she could easily forgive him. Although, she might let him suffer a little bit, as he deserved. But—and this was very possible—if Carrie was mistaken, then Rafe had just been making mischief. Tuck would have to be careful. Otherwise, she could make a fool of herself and perhaps ruin their friendship, and she didn't think she could bear that.

She sighed. If only the snow would let up soon. Otherwise, the Christmas dance would be cancelled, and there would go her dreams. Dreams of dancing, lightly and romantically, across the dance floor, in Rafe's arms, her dress billowing like a cloud and his eyes staring into hers adoringly.

She gave a chuckle. This confinement must be doing things to her mind. She returned to the kitchen to see Addy making loaves and placing them in the pans to rise again. They needed to get them all baked before Ma woke up from her nap. Otherwise she'd insist on doing it herself, and she tired so easily nowadays.

Addy gave her a sideways glance, and Tuck grinned. "Sorry. Guess I'm a little fidgety."

"I'll say," Addy said. "I don't blame you though. I'm getting cabin fever myself."

"I hope we won't have a bad winter. I don't think I could stand months of this." They'd had winters they'd been cooped up for weeks on end, with maybe a day here or there when they could escape the confines of the house.

"Remember the year we were snowed in with Great-Aunt Kate for a whole week?" Addy rolled her eyes and made a face.

Tuck chuckled. They'd been nine at the time and still getting used to being part of the Sullivan and Rayton families. "How could I forget? Uncle Will threatened to tan our hides, and Ma told him if there was any hide tanning to be done Papa Jack was more than capable of doing it."

"Yes, then Aunt Sarah got all over Ma for daring to be so mean." Addy giggled. "Those two boys of theirs are worse than we ever were."

"Hmm. I'm not sure of that. We were pretty ornery."

Addy nodded. "So, what would you rather have? A little sister or brother?"

"I'm not sure if it matters. All babies look like little toads for the first few months anyway." At least all of them she'd ever seen.

"Abby. That's terrible." Addy's mouth twisted, and a laugh exploded from her mouth. "They do look funny at first. But they're sweet. I plan to have at least three someday."

"You do?" She'd never thought of Addy as a mother. She picked up the dishrag and started wiping the table down.

"Of course. Don't you?" Addy raised an eyebrow in her direction. She opened the oven door and placed a pan of bread inside, then reached for another.

Tuck stood and stared at her sister. "I've never thought about it."

"Really? I think about it all the time." She wiped her hands on her apron. "Do you think four loaves will be enough?"

"Huh? Oh. Yes." She eyed her sister. "Who do you think of as the father?"

"Well, when we were in eighth grade, I used to think about marrying Joe Smith, but then he moved away. Since then, no one. I just think about my children." She gazed at Tuck. "You should think about it, Abby."

"I don't know if I'd be a good mother."

"Sure you will." Addy grinned. "And Rafe'll be a wonderful father."

Heat washed over Tuck's head and ran all the way down to her toes. "What if I don't marry Rafe?"

Addy's eyes held hers, and she smiled. "You will. You know you will."

She thought she would. Yes, she knew she would. Or was it just wishful thinking?

&.

Rafe dug the long-handled shovel down into the drifted snow and scooped the last of the piled-up snow to the side of the path. The heavy winds had lasted for nearly three days.

Snow had fallen steadily for four, finally dwindling down to next to nothing this morning. He'd breathed a sigh of relief and wasted no time clearing a path from the side porch to the barn. He'd been trudging through the cold, wet depths every day to take care of the animals. Pa was up and around now and couldn't wait to get busy again.

Rafe stepped inside and looked around at the contented animals. Must be nice. He chuckled at the ridiculous thought. They'd all been fed earlier and the cows milked. His sight drifted up to the rafters and rested on the pair of sleigh runners. He and Pa had repaired and oiled them at the end of winter last year. They never knew when they'd have to use them to get around. Either that or wait until the snow melted to get needed supplies.

However, Rafe had another purpose in mind. He'd removed the buggy wheels a couple of days ago. Now all he'd have to do is attach the runners. He climbed up in the loft and reached for the sharp runners, lifting them down carefully, one by one.

He had them fitted on the buggy, when the door opened and Pa stepped in, bundled up from head to feet. Ma's doing, more than likely. "I figured that's what you were up to out here," Pa cackled, his voice still a little hoarse. "So this is the big day I take it?"

Rafe nodded. "If I can get Tuck to go with me for a ride, I intend to ask her, Pa."

Pa squeezed Rafe's shoulder. "God go with you, son. I'll be praying. If Tuck loves you, she'll say yes."

Rafe swallowed past the lump that had suddenly formed. "And if she doesn't?"

"Then it's best you find out now, so you can quit pining and wait for the right one." He turned. "You'd best get some blankets to take along. Don't want the girl to freeze while you're popping the question."

"No, that wouldn't be good." Rafe laughed then sobered. "Thank you for your prayers, Pa. I don't know if I've ever told you, but knowing you and Ma pray for me has always given me comfort."

"You haven't told me, but I knew. I had a praying ma myself. No telling where I'd be today if it wasn't for her prayers." He reached a hand up and wiped at his eyes. "Guess I got something in my eye."

❧

Soon Rafe was gliding across the rolling farmland. His mouth was dry and his face numb. From the cold? Or the uncertainty of what was to come?

He stopped the horses alongside the front porch, and before he was out of the transformed buggy, the door was flung open and Jack stepped outside, holding the door open for him. Good sign. At least Jack was still friendly.

A moment later, he stood in the parlor greeting Lexie and the girls. Addy grinned and said hello.

After looking at everything in the room but him, Tuck finally looked him in the eye. "Hi, Rafe."

"Abigail, why don't you get Rafe something hot to drink? He looks half frozen." Lexie sat in a rocker with a blanket over her lap. She pursed her lips and smiled.

"No thank you, ma'am. I don't want anything to drink. I really came to see if Tuck wants to go for a sleigh ride."

"Oh, but it's terribly cold out there." Lexie frowned and glanced at Tuck.

"I didn't get cold at all, ma'am. There are plenty of blankets, and Ma sent hot water bottles for our feet. . ." He darted a glance at Tuck. "That is, if she wants to."

Her eyes widened as she stared at him. Then she jumped up. "I'd like to go for a sleigh ride. That is, if you won't worry, Ma. I'll be fine."

Lexie reluctantly agreed, and soon Rafe drove down the

lane, with Tuck swaddled in coats and blankets and her small feet placed on the hot water bottles.

"Thanks for coming with me, Tuck. I really need to talk to you about something." How to begin?

"Uh-huh. It wouldn't by any chance have something to do with Carrie Sue, would it?"

"Err. . .sort of. That is. . .I was teasing about her." He cleared his throat. "She's a nice girl, but not for me."

"Yes, so I discovered." She turned and glared at him.

His stomach roiled. She knew. How? Who could have gotten to her in this weather and blabbed before he had a chance to talk to her? "I'm sorry, Tuck. I don't know what got into me." Pure orneriness? And a little bit of revenge?

"I felt like a fool when I found out the truth. I was going to offer to help her plan the wedding." Her teeth chattered. "What if I had? It's a good thing Addy saw her in town that day."

"You were going to help her plan the wedding? When you thought she was marrying me?"

"It was all I could think of to do for you, Rafe." Her face was like stone. "For all I knew, Carrie wouldn't want us to be friends anymore. I thought if I became her friend, too, she wouldn't mind."

His heart sank. "So you want things to go on like they've always been between us?"

She turned her head and looked away. Her breath rose and fell in gasps.

"Tuck? Is that what you want?"

"It's what you want, isn't it?" The sob in her voice was unmistakable.

Why couldn't he breathe? He took a deep, slow breath. "Look at me, Tuck."

She shook her head, and her shoulders shook.

He put his hand on her shoulder and turned her around.

Her eyes swam with tears, and he took one finger and wiped them away. "No." He could barely get the words out. "It's not what I want."

The hope in her eyes met the hope in his heart. "What do you want, Rafe?" she whispered.

"I want you to be my wife," he croaked out.

She let out a *whoosh* of air and glared. "Just like that? I don't get to be courted first? Even Carrie gets to be courted. You almost courted her yourself."

"Tuck, calm down. Of course I'll come courting. We can't possibly get married before spring anyways. Our mas wouldn't hear of it. Do you always have to argue about everything?"

She turned her face up and looked him full in the face, her eyes dancing with mischief. "Not always."

His breath caught, and then he laughed. "I'm so glad."

He lowered his head and met her waiting lips.

epilogue

May 10, 1902

Tuck stood in the small Sunday school room at the front of the church.

Ma adjusted Tuck's lacy veil and tucked in a straying lock of hair. A baby cried in the sanctuary. Ma smiled and kissed Tuck on the cheek. "I love you, Abigail."

Tuck grinned. "I love you, too, Ma, but I think you'd better go take care of my baby sister."

Ma laughed, a bubbling, joy-filled laugh, and headed for the door. "I think you're right. Princess Elizabeth calls."

Finally, Tuck was alone with Addy, whose face was joyful and forlorn all at once.

The piano signaled it was time for Addy to precede Tuck down the aisle. Addy smiled. "That's for me. The next time we speak, you'll be Mrs. Rafe Collins."

Tuck leaned forward and gave her a hug, then turned her around. She slipped a gold chain around Addy's neck and fastened the clasp, letting the locket drop down across the bodice of her soft blue dress. "This is yours, sis. It's always been yours. I just borrowed it for a while."

Addy gasped and clutched the locket. "Oh, Abby. Are you sure?"

"Very sure. Remember? We agreed. Grandfather's violin was mine and mother's locket was yours. I've always loved my fiddle more."

"But it's the only picture we have of our mother."

"I can still see it, silly. We'll always be close together."

A moment later, her twin stepped from the room and walked down the aisle.

Mrs. Jenkins struck a chord. Tuck breathed deeply then stepped out and took Papa Jack's arm.

Her heart raced as she took the first step then calmed as she focused on Rafe standing next to Jim, his best man. As she walked toward him, he smiled and his eyes adored her, just as they did in the dream. They weren't dancing this time, but she wore a beautiful dress that billowed like a cloud.

Papa Jack kissed her cheek and placed her hand in Rafe's, then went to sit down.

"Dearly beloved, we are gathered together, to join this man and this woman in holy matrimony. . ."

Tuck turned to Rafe and found his waiting eyes filled with love. Her Rafe. Her darling best friend.

A Letter To Our Readers

Dear Reader:

In order that we might better contribute to your reading enjoyment, we would appreciate your taking a few minutes to respond to the following questions. We welcome your comments and read each form and letter we receive. When completed, please return to the following:

Fiction Editor
Heartsong Presents
PO Box 719
Uhrichsville, Ohio 44683

1. Did you enjoy reading *White River Song* by Frances Devine?
   ❏ Very much! I would like to see more books by this author!
   ❏ Moderately. I would have enjoyed it more if

   _____

   _____

   _____

2. Are you a member of **Heartsong Presents**? ❏ Yes ❏ No
   If no, where did you purchase this book? _____

   _____

3. How would you rate, on a scale from 1 (poor) to 5 (superior), the cover design? _____

4. On a scale from 1 (poor) to 10 (superior), please rate the following elements.

   ____ Heroine   ____ Plot
   ____ Hero   ____ Inspirational theme
   ____ Setting   ____ Secondary characters

5. These characters were special because? _____
_____
_____

6. How has this book inspired your life? _____
_____
_____

7. What settings would you like to see covered in future
   Heartsong Presents books? _____
_____
_____

8. What are some inspirational themes you would like to see
   treated in future books? _____
_____
_____

9. Would you be interested in reading other **Heartsong
   Presents** titles? ❑ Yes ❑ No

10. Please check your age range:
   ❑ Under 18   ❑ 18-24
   ❑ 25-34   ❑ 35-45
   ❑ 46-55   ❑ Over 55

Name _____
Occupation _____
Address _____
City, State, Zip _____
E-mail _____

A Bride's
PORTRAIT

OF DODGE CITY, KANSAS

Deputy Miles Carr has his hands full trying to keep the peace in Dodge City and find a local shopkeeper's killer. When his inquiries lead him to the door of Addie Reid's photography studio, he finds himself more than a little distracted. Does this beauty hold the clue to the killer's identity?

Historical, paperback, 320 pages, 5.5" x 8.375"

Hearts❤ng

Presents

Great Inspirational Romance
at a Great Price!

Heartsong Presents books are inspirational romances in contemporary and historical settings, designed to give you an enjoyable, spirit-lifting reading experience. You can choose wonderfully written titles from some of today's best authors like Wanda E. Brunstetter, Mary Connealy, Susan Page Davis, Cathy Marie Hake, Joyce Livingston, and many others.

When ordering quantities less than six, above titles are $3.99 each.
Not all titles may be available at time of order.